AF098000

Dear Friends

SHORT STORIES BY
Greg Stioham

PathBinder
Publishing

Published by PathBinder Publishing
P.O. Box 2611
Columbus, IN 47202
www.PathBinderPublishing.com

Copyright © 2021 by Greg Stidham
All rights reserved

Edited by Sullivan Alexander
Cover designed by Anna Perlich
Author photo by Peter Hendra/Kingston Whig-Standard

First published in 2021

Manufactured in the United States

ISBN: 978-1-955088-14-5
Library of Congress Control Number: 2021922538

All rights reserved. No part of this book may be reproduced or transmitted in any form whatsoever without prior written permission from the publisher except in the case of brief quotations embodied in critical articles and reviews.

These stories and their characters are all fictional; any resemblance to actual events or individuals is purely coincidental.

Introduction

I have a good friend who several years ago lost her husband. He had been ill for more than a year with slow, but relentless deterioration. They had time to prepare together for his death, and when that time came they both seemed to accept what they'd long known was coming. She seemed sad, of course, but accepting, at peace even.

When we talked some time later, she recounted a number of experiences that she thought were meaningful – feeling his presence in the room, hearing his voice. She included even talking with me and my wife about our mutual memories of her husband, my friend. And she said to us, "There are no coincidences in this life." I know what she meant – that there is a design to all that happens to us, some "greater power" overseeing all and orchestrating much. I was not eager to embrace much of the supernatural implications of her comments, but I am now reminded of them, however obliquely, and of why I wrote and chose to share these short stories.

I have been struck by how important encounters with other people can be or become. Many times these are chance encounters with strangers, but under circumstances that seem to elevate the encounters to something more. These, I believe, coincidences or not, are special moments that are frequently missed, not recognized, not appreciated. All that is required is fully opened eyes. Haven't we all had such encounters, recognized or missed?

This notion is what gave birth to the stories in this collection. A middle aged man with a progressive neurological disorder encounters a young, troubled girl during a long bus ride; they develop a relationship during a short portion of their temporarily overlapping journeys.

An isolated man experiences his first seizure, which brings him to the brink of his personal history, his belief system, his regrets. A chance encounter with a similarly flawed chaplain leads to the promise of a friendship and a truce with his personal demons.

A young mother loses her only child, a toddler who drowns in a tragic accident. Her journey to recovery includes utmost despair, reconciliation with her parents, and eventually a journey to find the boy's father.

These stories are all quite different from one another, but they share one thread. They all embrace flawed people brave enough to accept chance encounters, with eyes wide open. My hope is that they entertain, but also remind us all to engage in "chance" encounters with eyes wide open.

Table of Contents

Introduction iii

Trip to St. Vitus 7
Salvation Army 17
Asystole 31
Music 101 37
The Kid and the Poet 69
Homecoming 77
Bus Ride to Minot 83
Coming Home 109
Group 119
Fairbanks 139

Acknowledgments 163
About the Author 164

TRIP TO ST. VITUS

Pine-Sol slipped up his nostrils before he was awake. The strong, clean scent was good. It burned a bit, and it made his nose twitch in the slumber of early morning toward the end of a night's sleep. But it smelled good, and it made him feel good about the cleanness of the air he breathed, still half dreaming. It was reassuring.

He didn't open his eyes, though through his lids he could make out the first of the morning light spilling in through the bedroom window. He allowed himself to ease back into dozing with the reassuring scent of the Pine-Sol growing ever stronger.

He didn't know how long he'd been back asleep when he heard it, but when he did, its pitch and intensity startled him awake. It was an air raid siren from the Second Great War, only louder. Or a tornado warning siren outside Topeka, only shriller. It was so loud that it was surely maiming his eardrums.

The Pine-Sol was stronger than ever, but it was unnoticeable with the unbearable sound in his ears. He tried to wake himself, but he couldn't. He thought if he moved an arm, perhaps to the side of the bed where it would fall toward the floor, perhaps then he would awaken from the movement. But his arm was heavy. Heavy as a bag of sand bought to fill a child's sandbox. He could not move the arm. He couldn't even budge it. He was trapped in his wakeful sleep, terrified.

Trapped in this sleep, paralyzed underwater, he was unable to move anything. He could move nothing that would help him wake up from what he knew had to be a dream. And the shrill scream of the siren would not stop. And the Pine-Sol continued to suffocate the membranes of his nostrils. He was trapped underwater, drowning, not able to move to wake up, but the light still filtered through his lids, and the water, creating shadows of everything around him. And the shrill scream of the siren kept piercing his ears.

He thought he was not dead, not dead yet. And he thought he might be able to muster enough will and enough strength to bring himself awake. If only he could concentrate hard enough. Surely enough mental strength could bring him through this, and out of this. And so he tried, concentrating, trying again to regain some movement in one arm. Nothing. And then the other. Again, nothing.

He tried and tried, and nothing would move. Not an arm. No leg. His eyelids, even. Though he could see light filtering dimly through, he could not lift the heavyweight eyelids that kept him from seeing the familiar things in his bedroom.

He was falling, sinking deeper into ocean waters, and the lights were getting dimmer, the water slightly darker, the shadows more ominous. He knew he had to concentrate now, harder than he'd ever had to before, and he decided on his eyelids. Like a heavyweight lifter, he concentrated on the barbells on the front of his face, concentrated on bench pressing them open, no matter how much it hurt, how much he feared failing. He concentrated, and he pushed with every muscle in his face, every muscle in his body, to lift those weights, even just a tiny bit.

He worked and worked until he thought he would faint, and then one more push — his eyelids came open. And there was light. Real light. From everywhere. He tried to move his arms, but they were still heavy as sandbags. He couldn't budge them. But there was light. He could turn his eyes toward his bedroom window where the sunlight poured in, and it was familiar. But not. It was not yellow, or white, like he remembered — it was fuchsia.

Blood-purple light filled the room, and everything in it. The walls were bathed in it. The door to the hallway dripped it, as did the ceiling. In the mirror on the dresser he could see his face. It too was fuchsia. And his hair. And still the siren pierced his ears, and the Pine-Sol played games with his nostrils.

At least he could move his eyes, from side to side, and up and down. But his arms and his legs felt like they'd been placed in concrete casts. He couldn't move them at all. He was terrified, and knew that he had to find some way to get out of bed. He also knew that his sheer strength of will had made it possible to get his eyes open.

So now he began to concentrate, focusing every bit of mental energy on bending his legs. For five minutes, or five hours, he concentrated. And then he pulled his left foot up in the bed, cocking his knee beneath the sheets. The effort exhausted him, but he continued to concentrate until his right knee was also bent.

The morning dragged on, and the fuchsia sunlight grew brighter streaming through the bedroom window. After a long while, he was able to move his arms and lift his head from the pillow. Then he worked his elbows behind his back and pushed himself up into a sitting position. He sat there for a long time, exhausted. Finally, he twisted to drop his legs over the side of the bed.

It must have been near lunchtime before he was able to put his feet on the floor and begin to try to bear weight. The siren's wail was less now, or he was getting used to it. Pine-Sol still permeated the air, making it clean and fresh. He wanted to get downstairs where things might be normal again.

Holding onto the head of the bed, he pulled himself to his feet, fully standing. The room reeled, circling around him. He felt like he was swimming, and he was nauseous. He thought he might have to throw up, so he steadied himself and stood still, taking deep breaths until the nausea faded and the spinning room slowed.

He knew he had to get down the stairs to his living room, and to the kitchen where the phone was. He summoned his strength now that the nausea was less, and began taking steps toward the door of the bedroom, and to the stairs just beyond.

The elation of success was surpassed only by surprise when he found he'd managed to make it to the head of the stairs. But the biggest challenge remained ahead: the fuchsia walls leading down the narrow single flight of stairs that seemed like an infinite descent into hell.

He took firm hold of the staircase. Very consciously planning every part of the move, he cautiously placed one foot on the first step leading down. The room gyrated briefly, but the second step seemed also possible. He took it. And one step at a time — one stairstep, and one footstep at a time — he slowly made his way down to the first floor.

When he got to the living room, he was exhausted, and he collapsed into the ancient recliner chair, a family relic from years past. But not before grabbing the cordless phone from the table next to the chair and calling his sister.

Later, he did not remember calling, or what he said. What he did remember was a sudden desire to do yoga in the fuchsia light bathing the room where he sat. And he remembered taking his foot, and bending his leg so his foot could be propped behind his neck. And he remembered almost succeeding. That was all he remembered.

***

Smokey's black nose hovered inches above his face, dripping occasional drops of clear, cool snot into his beard. The large shepherd, his best friend for a decade, looked down into his eyes. There was no fuchsia aura — just black nose, deep brown eyes, and clear drops of cool snot.

He tried to lift his head, so that he could touch his forehead to the dog's cool nose. But his head felt like a blacksmith's anvil when he tried to lift it. The headache pounded, and he closed his eyes until the pain lessened a bit. When he opened his eyes, the dog was gone.

***

"OK. I think we can take these pads off now."

He heard the loud, authoritative voice, and the next thing he knew he was a limp, shot rabbit in the hands of a knife-wielding hunter in the woods. He felt the skin being ripped from his hairy chest.

He let loose a loud profanity, his eyes started open wide, and the white sun blazed blindingly down on him from directly above where he lay on his back. He could make out the shadowy forms of faces surrounding him on both sides, and above his head. The one above his face leaned in so close he could smell his breath. Not Pine-Sol, but something else. Rubbing alcohol. Yes. It was rubbing alcohol.

"Mr. Novack. Mr. Novack. Can you hear me?" the face yelled so loudly it hurt his already-pained ears.

"How the hell can I not hear you? Turn your volume down!" he tried to say. But the words came out all jumbled, mumbled.

"Do you know where you are, Mr. Novack?" Apparently the face had not gotten the message about the damned volume. "You are in the Emergency Room at St. Vitus Medical Center. You had a seizure."

He thought they meant he'd been caught and they had seized drugs, but he didn't have any drugs. He didn't know what they meant.

"We're going to take you to Radiology for an MRI. Your sister is waiting just outside, and you can see her when you get back," the voice bellowed. And then everything was calm, silent darkness again.

The next time he opened his eyes, he was lying in a dark tunnel, and the sound of a jackhammer surrounded his head, pounding his ears. "Cow-chuka, cow-chuka, cow-chuka." He looked down and could see his feet silhouetted by a faint, bluish light coming from behind what appeared to be a glass window. He thought he could see too, just on the other side of the glass, the outline of a face looking in at him.

Was he dead? Was this hell? He didn't know what was going on, but he instantly felt remorse for bad things he'd done in his life.

He wondered, had he done everything he could to save his marriage? What about his son? Was he not paying enough attention when his son began smoking pot every day and flunked out of college? Those, and other thoughts, drifted through his mind as he drifted back into sleep to the rhythm of the "cow-chuka."

The next time he awoke, he was in a regular bed, one with a sturdy rail. Something was wrapped around his upper arm, and the wrap was tightening on its own, almost to where it hurt.

"Good morning, Mr. Novack. My name is Sandy, and I will be your nurse today. How are you feeling?"

"I don't know," he replied. "Where the hell am I?"

"You are in the hospital. You came in from Emergency yesterday evening. You've been sleeping pretty soundly ever since. Can I get you anything?"

"Can I get some cold water?" he answered.

"You sure can. I'll get it for you just as soon as I finish taking your vital signs." And with that, he fell back asleep, the tight arm wrap lightening quickly.

The next three days passed, it seemed quickly to him, but he wasn't sure. He slept most of the time, day and night. He was so exhausted he could not keep himself awake, could not concentrate enough to carry on a conversation with the nurses when they came in to check his vitals, or with his sister the one time she visited. He barely remembered talking with his landlord, who was also his friend.

He remembered a doctor coming in and standing next to his bed. The doctor told him his name, but he couldn't remember it. He did remember the doctor saying something about the MRI being normal, and medication, and epilepsy.

He remembered also that the bed next to his had been empty, and then some time later there was a man lying in it, older than he was. His roommate also was not awake, and he had a clear plastic tube coming out of his nose. Novack thought he should say hello, but also felt that he shouldn't wake him.

***

On the third day, during one of his longer wakeful spells, a man came into the room and approached his bed. He looked to be in his mid-sixties, with thinning white hair and bushy white eyebrows. His eyes sparkled from his round face, and he was wearing a black, straight-neck shirt with an opening in front that revealed a white collar underneath.

"Good morning, Mr. Novack. I'm Father McGurdy, the chaplain here, and I thought I'd drop in to see how you're feelin'."

"Hello," he replied.

Father McGurdy explained further, "Your papers say you're Catholic, so I thought I'd drop by to see if you wanted to chat, go to confession, receive communion, or if there'd be anything else I might do for you."

Novack was confused. Catholic? Yes, he guessed. He'd been Catholic once, but he hadn't been to mass in more than thirty years. And confession? Jesus. He hadn't been to confession since he was in grade school. He did remember his manners, though.

"Thank you, Father. I appreciate it. What did you say your name was?"

"McGurdy. Patrick McGurdy."

"I'm pleased to meet you, Father."

Father McGurdy held out his hand to shake Novack's, and responded with a question. "So, Mr. Novack. Tell me what brings you to St. Vitus."

"I'm not sure, Father. I think I went to hell."

"No, son. You only went to purgatory. It says in your papers that you had a seizure." And then, almost as an afterthought, he clarified, "I was just kiddin' about purgatory.

The nurses said you're gonna be okay."

"Well, thank God for that, eh Father?"

"Damn right about that, son."

Novack was reassured to hear the priest say "damn."

"So, Mr. Novack... Have you got any family in town?" the priest asked.

"Just my sister," he replied. "And I have two sons, but they live far away."

"What about your wife? Are you married? Oh, may I call you Charles?"

"Uh, no. I mean, yes. I mean, no, the wife left years ago. And yes, please do call me Charles."

Father McGurdy frowned slightly, nodded, then smiled and said, "Thanks. Nice to meet you, Charles. So, how might you be feelin' about havin' this epilepsy?"

13

"I dunno. I don't know what it is, exactly. It's pretty bad, but not as bad as being in hell, I guess."

"Ha!" Father chuckled. "No, indeed. But it might be a bit scary. Is it?"

"Well, Father... I'll tell ya. I was scared as shit for days. I mean for days!"

"And what was it that scared you, Charles? Were you scared o' dyin'?"

"Oh, no Father. I always thought dyin' was the easy part. It's living that tries the soul."

"Well," Father McGurdy responded thoughtfully. "I think you might be right about that." He paused. "So if not the dyin', what was it that scared you?"

A moment of silence filled the room. Then Novack said, "Hell, Father. It's hell that scares me."

"Hell scares the shit outta me, too, Charles. What is it about hell that scares you? You tell me, and I'll tell you."

"You're askin' me that, Father? Hell is what awaits sinners, right? Well, I ain't been to mass in a long, long time. I don't pray, not really. Not ever. I try to do good, but I'm not sure I have done so well."

Father McGurdy had a thoughtful, serious look. "What do you mean, Charles?"

"Father, I swear I did the best I could. I tried. But, well... I'm not sure I did so well. In fact, I think I fucked up more than I did good. It wasn't my plan. But I fucked up a lot more than I wish I had."

Father McGurdy was quiet. He pulled a chair up to the side of the bed, and he sat down. Still, he said nothing. He sat, arms crossed so one arm lay across his chest, the other, elbow bent, with his chin in his hand. He still said nothing.

"Father? You okay?"

"Yeah. I was just thinkin'. I don't know if I know anybody who didn't fuck up."

Neither man spoke for a long time. Father McGurdy sat with his chin in his hand, and Novack lay in his bed, half-propped to sitting, both men looking into the distance. Finally, Father McGurdy spoke.

"I don't know anybody who hasn't fucked up. But I know a few who tried not to fuck up." And he paused. "They tried hard to fuck up as little as possible, and maybe even to do a little good, along the way, for someone else."

And the two were silent again. Novack was confused, but not like before. He was confused by the priest's words. And then the priest spoke again.

"I think I fucked up, too. But I tried. I'd like to think that is what matters."

Another silence. "Charles, would you like to receive communion?"

"Oh, Father. I can't."

"Why not?"

Novack thought for a minute, then answered, "Because I haven't been to mass in over thirty years. And I haven't been to confession in a lot longer than that, and I know you are supposed to go to confession within two weeks before receiving communion."

"Charles. You just confessed."

Novack started upright. "Really?" he asked.

Father McGurdy's reply was quick. "Charles, you are ready to receive communion if you wish."

Novack thought for a moment, and then slowly said, "Yes, Father. I think I'd like that."

The priest took a small leather wallet from his small satchel, and opened it. From it he withdrew a small velvet package, unfolded it, and withdrew a small, white wafer. He held it before Novack, and pronounced the words, "Charles, behold the body of Christ."

Novack remembered the response. "Amen."

And he took the wafer and placed it into his mouth, softened it with his saliva as he'd been taught as an 8-year old, then swallowed it.

The two men were silent, and then Father McGurdy began to re-organize the leather wallet. He put the wallet in his satchel, and was slowly getting up, apparently preparing to move on to his next visit. Novack interrupted the slow, somber preparations.

"Father? I am supposed to get out of here tomorrow or the next day."

"Yes?"

"Well, there's a great Irish band playing at Murphy's Thursday. Would you let me buy you a beer?" Novack's voice was hesitant.

Father McGurdy looked him in the eye for a long moment, and he drew a deep breath. "Yeah. Murphy's. A beer. I'd love that, son. Murphy's. Thursday, then."

SALVATION ARMY

1

She was walking so briskly, quick-stepped, like those soldiers in old black-and-white World War II movies. They called it goose-stepping. Parades of the bad guys. I remember watching them on my grandpa's Magnavox. There would be fifteen or more, side by side, hundreds deep. Marching, kicking their legs up like college football cheerleaders today, looking to the side. They were scary.

She made me think of them, storming across the parking lot. Her heels were high, raising her up three inches. And they were loud, like cannon shots. I thought she might salute me. Or, worse, kick me. So instead of a salute, I rang my bells.

The bells were attached to a thin leather strap. The strap was so thin, I thought it might have been made for something else. I wasn't even sure it was leather. I wasn't sure about her at all, but I was determined not to flee, so I sat there and I rang the bells, as the clop-clop of her boots drew closer and closer. Her boot lifted her up to the step to where I sat, outside the door. She nearly knocked over my bucket, and just who would have been in trouble then?

The night air grew even colder as she stormed past through the automatic doors and into the warmth of the liquor store. While I watched, scratching my five o'clock shadow, she disappeared into the bright light of the aisle packed with bottles. My khaki winter jacket was losing its battle with the cold wind. And I shivered in my corner on the steps of the store, with my tripod-strapped kettle not so full of coins.

I jingled the bells again when two couples came up the step. I saw them. I know they looked, but they pretended they didn't.

They walked right by, with me jingling the non-leather strap of bells more and more frantically, hoping for a coin toss into my kettle. They pretended they didn't see, but I saw them. And they saw me.

I'm not sure how I was chosen for this job. It's a volunteer job, so I don't get money; but still, there were lots of others applying. I waited with a small group. We were all waiting to get the paperwork we would have to fill out. I looked at all of them. There were businessmen. A young mother carrying a small kid on one arm. Some older folks who looked like they'd just wandered away from their forever home.

And there was me. I never made it through high school. You see, I was what they called "special." So I got to take special classes, with other kids who were special, too. And I did real well. Fifth grade all the way up to eighth. I got the best grades you could get.

When I started high school, everything was different. It was really hard. The classes were hard, and the subjects were hard, too. But what was really hard were the teachers. If they said something we needed to learn, but they said it too fast, we couldn't just ask them to say it again, more slowly, like we could in the school before.

The new school was hard for other reasons, too. When I left my old school, I also left my friends. Maybe I will see them again someday, but I don't know. Before, I could always count on them, and now they weren't there anymore.

In the new school it was different. People didn't really make friends. Some had their own small groups, but they didn't ever say anything to me. Sometimes, though, they made remarks, and laughed, pointing in my direction.

My grades weren't good anymore either, and by the end of my second year at the new school, I decided to quit. Now I live in the basement room of my mom and dad's, so I don't need a whole lot of money. I got a job cleaning the floors at night at my old school, my special school. Not much money, but enough for the bus and for the *Three Musketeers* movie.

I didn't think they would take me for this job, but the thought of wearing a Santa cap and ringing a bell to make money for poor people seemed like a great idea. They helped me fill out the papers, and a few days later, my mom called for me downstairs and said I had a phone call. It was the lady from the Salvation Army. She told me that I had been chosen to be one of their volunteers. I was so excited I almost tripped on the basement stairs.

It's been two weeks now since my first night. After I got the job, my mom drove me to the office where I picked up my white-trimmed red cap, my kettle and the stand. I tried the cap on every day before I started, just to be sure it fit just right.

I was assigned to the liquor store about a mile from my house, three nights a week, until New Year's Day. Every morning after work, I was to bring the money I'd gotten to the office. I guess they just trusted me that I wouldn't take any for myself.

On my nights to work, I was to start at six in the evening and stay until the store closed at ten. Wednesday, Friday and Saturday. That would be my schedule for the next four weeks. That first night was one of the coldest. You could see your breath floating away from your lips.

I was so excited I was nervous, and I set up my chair in the corner outside the door, my kettle in the tripod. I rang my bells for the first time. Most of the time I sat waiting for people to walk by. When they did, I would ring my bells. And when I had to pee, the store people let me use the washroom in the back. Of course, I had to bring my kettle with me. When people passed, leaving the store, I rang the bell, and I got some coins from a few of the people. It wasn't as much as I thought, but I guess okay for my first night.

The night I saw the goose-stepping lady was the Wednesday before Christmas. That was not one of the good nights. Everyone was in a hurry, or in a bad mood. I wished them all "Merry Christmas" when they passed, but for the most part, they looked the other way, and then hurried on without saying anything, bags in their arms. A few people pressed coins into the slot in the top of my kettle.

One guy stuffed his chewing gum into the slot. I think he was trying to make me mad. But it didn't work. I just dug the gum out with my fingernail after he went on to his car.

The goose-stepping woman stayed in the store a long time, longer than most of the customers. When the electric sliding doors hummed open to let her pass, I immediately heard the clop-clop of her heels again. She had a large bag under each arm. I rang my bells and said "Merry Christmas," while she sternly turned her head to the side and silently snarled at me.

A few more customers passed by on the way in to the warmth of the store, and then back out into the darkness of the parking lot. A man and his wife passed by, and she dropped a coin into my kettle.

Three college girls giggled past. When they came out, two of them dropped a handful of coins into the bucket. I thanked them and wished them "Merry Christmas." Most of the customers just passed by. I was invisible, even though I rang the bells.

Just before it was time for the store to close, an old woman rode up the walk in a 3-wheeled electric scooter. It was red, with a little pennant flag on a stick. She had a pack on the back of the seat with a clear plastic hose coming out of it, leading around her side and up into her nose. I wasn't sure she would get over the step to the landing where I sat, but her scooter climbed right over it like an army tank. And the doors opened themselves, so they were not a problem. I rang my bells and said "Merry Christmas." She just glared at me.

The old lady on the scooter was in the store for only a few minutes. When she rolled through the opening doors she was already tipping a bag-wrapped bottle to her lips. As she passed me, I repeated my "Merry Christmas." Glaring at me again, in a voice as hoarse as a rusty saw blade, she spat, "Go to hell."

When the time came, the workers in the store dimmed the lights and began to leave the store, one by one. That was my signal to start packing up, too. After unlocking the chain that tethered my bike to the pole in the corner of the parking lot, I walked back to my corner just as the manager was locking the door. I wished him "Merry Christmas," and he said "Same to you," even though I am pretty sure he didn't celebrate Christmas. He spoke with an accent and I heard the other workers say he was from Iran.

After getting my bike, I put my kettle into the basket on my handlebars. And I folded up the tripod stand and strapped it to the back of my seat, got on the bike, and began to pedal off into the dark.

The first part of my ride home took me down a dark road past an apartment complex. You could never be sure who might be there, during the day or the night. I was usually not afraid. I had ridden my bike by there many times, even when I was a kid. It was a little different at night, though, and my pedaling was a bit more brisk, my Santa cap perched precariously on my head.

"Where the hell do you think you're going?" The voice came from the dark just as I was turning a corner. Then I made out in front of me a young man, or teenager, bundled in an army jacket. And then I saw two more guys standing behind him.

"Home," I said. "I just got off work."

He snorted. "And where do you work? The North Pole?" I guess he noticed the Santa cap.

"No. At the liquor store."

"Liquor store. You got any booze with you?"

"No, sir."

He stepped closer, eyeing my bike. "What you got in the bucket there?"

"I was collecting money for Salvation Army. For poor people."

He laughed. "Well, aren't you lucky! You just found yourself some poor people. Why don't you just hand that little bucket over to these poor people?"

I felt myself start to shake as the three drew closer. "I can't do that. It is not mine to give away."

It was just then that the sky went white with lightning. And that was the last thing I remember.

2

Desirée was the last one to leave the office, and she knew she would have to hurry or she would be late for the Christmas dinner party. It was at his house, and she knew his wife would be there. And she, on the other hand, would have to act like she was just one of the other people in the office. Even worse, she would have to watch him chatting with his wife, having fun, being a real couple like *she* wanted to be with him. She was not in a good mood.

She walked briskly to her car in the cold air and scolded herself for not wearing her warmer winter jacket. There was no snow yet, but it felt like it couldn't be far away. She unlocked her Lexus with the remote. It was already dark and it wasn't even six o'clock yet.

She needed to stop by the liquor store and pick up a bottle of good wine to bring to the party. Then she would barely have time to get home, shower, fix her hair, and change into something that might at least grab his attention. Desirée was thinking about all of this when she pulled into the lot of the liquor store, got out, and walked hurriedly to the door.

She barely noticed the kid as she passed. He shook some toy bells and mumbled something as she passed, but she didn't quite catch it. And that ridiculous, faded Santa cap that looked like it was on its twentieth and last Christmas.

Desirée found the wine she was looking for, her favorite — a local Baco Noir. She grabbed two bottles and marched up to the checkout aisle. There were two people in front of her, so she had her debit card and Air Miles card ready when her turn came. After she paid, she put the bag in her arm and hurried out the automatic door.

This time she heard him. "Merry Christmas." But he was begging for money. She glared at him and walked briskly past and on to her car. She was not in a good mood.

3

They finished their last exams of the semester that day, and it was time to party before everyone packed up and headed back to their families and homes for the holidays. Roberta, or Robbie as her friends called her, and her two housemates were going to a party at the Gary's house. Gary was a good-looking guy in her Art History class. If the other guys coming to this party were half as cute as Gary, the girls were in for a good night.

Robbie got to their house around supper time. She had to shower and get dressed before her housemates laid claim to the bathroom. She had some new skinny jeans and a silk blouse she planned to wear. Both the jeans and the blouse were just revealing enough.

As she stripped off her sweatshirt and grungy jeans, she headed to the shower and called to her roommates. "Can someone order a pizza so we don't totally starve before the party?"

"Great idea!" came the reply from downstairs.

Robbie was from Vancouver. Both her roommates were from Toronto. The next morning they were all three taking the bus to Toronto which left from campus and goes straight to the airport. Robbie would then catch her plane west, and the other two would be met by their families.

Robbie scurried, towel-wrapped, from the bathroom to her bedroom. Her suitcase lay open on her bed, half-filled with clothes for her trip home. She moved it to the side and began to rummage through the underwear drawer of her dresser, finally choosing a matching pair of panties and bra. You just never knew who might get to see them tonight.

While she was pulling on the skinny jeans and buttoning her shirt, the doorbell announced the arrival of the pizza. Lanni called out, "I got it."

Robbie fastened her jeans and skipped down the stairs, bursting into the kitchen. She fished her wallet from her purse and handed a ten to Lanni to cover her portion of the pizza. "I'm starved!" And she grabbed a piece. Lannie and Claire both took a paper plate and loaded them with two pieces each before scurrying up the stairs to ready themselves for the party, and Robbie grinned thinking about Gary.

It was long past dark by the time the girls were ready to head out the door. All three were giggling with excitement as they skipped down the sidewalk. Before they got close to the liquor store, they broke out in song: "What do you do with a drunken sailor, what do you do with a drunken sailor..."

As they stepped up to the door of the store, Robbie noticed the young man with a Santa cap. As they passed, he rang his bells and said, "Merry Christmas." Once inside, they wandered the aisles, weighing their choices. Robbie picked up a six-pack of wine coolers, while Claire grabbed a bottle of Fireball cinnamon whiskey.

Robbie was the only one of the three with a credible fake ID, so she took all three items and made the purchase. She paid the clerk and kept the coins in her hand as the three of them left. As she passed the man with the Santa cap, she dropped the change into his kettle. Claire fished some coins out of her coat pocket, and dropped them in as well.

The man rang his bells. "Thank you. And Merry Christmas."

Then they were off down the road to Gary's house, singing again. They were going to have some fun tonight!

4

Old Miss Ratchett finished her supper in the dining area, pushing her plate to the center of the table where she sat with three other old women. Rachel had had a stroke. Her left arm was weak and her mouth drooped. She had to use a walker, too, but her mind was clear. She was one of the women who played canasta every afternoon in the parlor room.

Mrs. Taylor had been an opera singer when she was young. She still liked to sing around the home, but you couldn't understand the words. She had early dementia, and although she could still take pretty good care of herself, she couldn't carry on a coherent conversation if she had to.

Of all the people in the home, Norma Smythe had the most visitors. She had two sons and a daughter, and they all lived in town. All three of them had several children, and someone would come visit every afternoon and they would always bring some of the kids to visit as well. Norma was the most sociable of the residents. Nobody in the home had ever once seen a single person visit Miss Ratchett.

"You going out again tonight, Hazel?" Norma asked.

Miss Ratchett put her scooter in reverse and backed away from the table. "None of your goddamned business," she snarled, and lurched her scooter forward and down the hallway to her room. When she got there, she retrieved her jacket from the chair and, after removing the oxygen tubing from her nose, she twisted herself into it. Then she brought the tubing back around to the front and placed the prongs in her nose.

"Goddamned busybodies," she mumbled under her breath. She pulled her stocking cap down over her ears and pivoted the scooter in a perfect 180 degree turn, heading back out down the hallway to the front door. When she got there, one of the aides, a young Jamaican woman, opened the door and held it for her.

"Have a nice evening, Miss Ratchett."

"It'll be another shit evening, just like every other one in this hellhole." And off she whirred down the sidewalk.

Her scooter scooted faster than most people walked, and she was at the liquor store in no time. The step up to the door didn't slow her down. She knew exactly how to boost her scooter over it. "Oh, shit. Another one of those asshole beggars." She scooted on by, barely taking note of the Santa cap and kettle.

Jack Daniels. Jack Daniels. She knew just where it was. She whirred right over to the wall where it sat on the shelf waiting for her.

"Hey. Hey, you. You work here? Come grab this bottle for me."

The clerk came over, took the bottle off the shelf, and handed it to her. "'Bout time."

"Merry Christmas."

"Up yours."

And Miss Ratchet pivoted and headed toward the checkout line. She doled out her bills, took her change, said nothing when the clerk wished her a good night, and headed off into the dark outside the automatic door.

The young man was still there jingling his bells. "Merry Christmas." Goddamn. *This stupid kid is* still *saying Merry Christmas. Goddamn.*

5

Julio was bored as shit. His video games were not interesting any more. His mother had already left for one of her appointments. And he was alone in his filthy room, with his dirty clothes thrown all around with a few partly empty bags of chips. He found his nearly empty vodka bottle and poured what was left into a fruit juice glass.

He downed the vodka in a swallow, and pulled his cell phone from his backpack. Johnny would be home by now. Johnny was always up for fun, as long as there was some weed involved.

"Hey, Johnny. What's up?"

"Oh, nothin'. I just got home."

"So what are you doing tonight? Anything fun?"

"No. Nothing goin' on. Mom's gone. Place is empty as fuck. What about you?"

Julio thought a moment. "I was thinking about going out and looking for some babes. What do you say?"

Julio didn't know his father. All his life he was trailing after his mother. She worked all kinds of jobs. Waited tables in Alberta. Cleaned motel rooms outside of Saskatoon. Most of her jobs kept her away, sometimes for twelve hours or more. He went to school. A little. But he was never in one place long enough to fit in. Kingston was the longest they'd stayed in one place for as long as he remembered. But it really wasn't any different.

Since they moved to Kingston, his mother had started working longer hours, and at weirder times of day. Or night. In the day, she would tell him she was leaving for a job and would be back in a few hours. In the night, she would just leave.

"I've got some good weed. What say we go smoke and head out looking for babes? Or whatever action looks cool."

Johnny said, "Yeah. Sounds good. Meet at your place? Okay if I bring little Charlie along? He's feeling a bit lonely tonight." Charlie was Johnny's 13-year old kid brother.

"Sure. Bring him along. It's not like it's x-rated or anything."

They met up at the fence outside the housing project. Julio had the weed. A couple of joints. They set up in the corner of a parking lot. It was cold, but they all wore their jackets. Julio lit up first, inhaled, and passed the joint to Johnny as he exhaled smoke into the night.

"Hey, Charlie. You've smoked before, right? Just inhale and hold it in your lungs for a minute or so." Johnnie passed the joint to Charlie. The boy inhaled deeply, and immediately burst into a fit of coughing.

"Charlie, don't inhale so fast. Take a little, with a little air. You'll get used to it." Johnnie tried to be a good big brother.

They passed the joint around the circle three more times before there was nothing left. Charlie did okay after the first try. And then Julio lit up the second. It too was passed around the warming circle three times before its glow dimmed. The boys were all quite buzzed by this time. And talkative.

Julio said, "I hate my father." And then, "I don't even know who he is. I never even saw the bastard."

Johnny grunted. "Yeah. I knew my dad. He was an asshole. He beat my mom, and he beat me. And he would have beat Charlie if he'd stuck around long enough."

They started walking, passing through the fence gate toward the sidewalk beyond.

"Hey. Look at that dork on the bicycle. What is he, one of Santa's elves?" All three broke out in laughter.

Julio continued. "Hey, you two want to have some fun with this retard?"

"Yea. Watch this." Johnny stepped to the curb where the bike wobbled a few yards away.

"Where the hell do you think you're going?"

6

The voice was familiar. A deep voice with a slight rasp. I tried to open my eyes, and through the slit in one eye I could see a bright light. And then I saw my father's face looming over me, and heard his voice calling my name. My head hurt. And my ribs felt like a horse was sitting on me. I started to cry. I tried not to, but I couldn't help it.

"Where am I? What happened?"

My father's face grimaced. "You got attacked on your way home from collecting. When you didn't get home, I went looking for you. I found you on the side of the road down by the housing projects. You were out cold. They wanted to keep you in the hospital overnight."

"Where's my coin kettle?"

"You didn't have anything with you."

"What about my bike?"

My father shook his head. I started to cry again. "They took the money? And they took my bike?"

"Yes, son. I'm afraid they did."

I could barely see my father through my partly opened eye, and my other eye was swollen shut. My father looked like he wanted to cry with me.

"It's okay, son. It's gonna be okay."

"But, what about the money for the poor people?"

"It's okay, son, there's plenty of money been raised for them. Why you yourself raised a couple of hundred dollars!"

It was true. I had averaged twenty dollars a night. But what I lost was twenty *more* dollars I could have given to the poor people. I started to cry again, and I could feel the snot run down my upper lip.

"Son, it's okay. You did more than your share. You shouldn't worry about that. You should be taking care of your bruised face, black eye and broken ribs." And then as an afterthought, he added, "Are you upset about your bike?"

I didn't know how I would get to my job at the school now. Or anywhere else, for that matter. I started to cry again.

"I'll figure something out, Dad. The bike was mine, and I'll figure something out. But the money wasn't, and I was supposed to be taking care of it." *The Salvation Army people will be mad at me.*

"Dad, will you do something for me?"

"Sure, son. You name it. Anything."

I took a deep breath. "Dad, I have some money I've saved from my school job. It's in the top drawer of the desk in my room. Could you get twenty dollars and take it to the Salvation Army office over on Princess Street?"

"Sure, son. I'm glad to do it. I'm just glad you are okay." My father sighed.

"I'm going to head home and check in with your mom, and then I'll take the money over and let them know you won't be collecting for a while. Your mom and I will be back to see you after supper."

"Thanks, Dad."

My father got up and turned to leave.

"Dad?"

He paused and turned back toward me.

"Merry Christmas, Dad."

ASYSTOLE

Cliff pulled into one of the parking spaces in the lot below the row of condominiums, turned off the ignition, and opened the driver door of the five-year-old hatchback. The frigid air stung his cheeks. The first week after Christmas had brought the first real cold snap of winter, and temperatures had dropped to the low teens before Cliff had even left work. And now snow clouds hid the moon. The concrete stairway up to the condo doors was lit only by ornamental street lamps.

Cliff rolled out of the driver's seat and he closed the door behind him, hiking toward the steps while glancing at his watch in the glare beneath the closest light globe — just past 11:30. He knew his son would be asleep, and his wife too, with one wine bottle down and another half to go. At least he could look forward to five hours' sleep before getting up for work in the morning.

Cliff carefully climbed the concrete steps, glazed with a cobbled layer of ice. At the top, he took a breath, and spit onto the walk. He got to the door where he fumbled through his keys under the parking lot lights. When he found the right one, he opened his front door. Stepping into the bright foyer, he saw Darlene's angry face, Ryan screaming in her bouncing arms.

"Where the hell have you been? We are out of milk and juice both, and Ryan's gone out of control!"

Cliff tossed his backpack onto the couch. "Okay. I'll run down to the 7-Eleven and pick up some milk. You want juice, too?"

"Well, what sense does it make for you to go down there and not get both?"

Cliff zipped his jacket back up and headed to the door. The cold air hit him in the face as soon as he stepped back into the dim light and closed the door behind him. Most nights were like this if Darlene were not already snoring. She snapped at him as soon as he walked through the door.

Cliff could not be blamed for his late hours. That was just part of being a medical resident. Also part of the reason he sometimes looked forward to his nights on call at the hospital.

When Cliff got home at a decent hour, he wanted nothing more than to fall to the floor and play with Ryan. Toy trucks held center stage, but airplanes were starting to come on strong. It didn't matter if it was the day after an "all-nighter" at the hospital. No matter how tired, Cliff needed his time with Ryan.

Before Ryan, there had been time with Darlene. She certainly had her own friends, and when Cliff was on call, she would have a "girls' night out." When he was not on call or in the languor of post-call fatigue, Darlene would be energetic and affectionate. She would have made burgers or spaghetti, which may or may not get finished before the two would find themselves in the bedroom, creating disarray of their Queen-sized waterbed.

That was before Ryan. Soon after Ryan's birth, Darlene slipped into a depression. She went early to bed and stayed in bed late, and not to frolic. Cliff rejoiced at those moments, even though sex was now becoming a fading memory, replaced by Darlene's anger. Soon it was also replaced by the alcohol.

Cliff took a deep breath as he walked back toward the concrete steps. Tonight's brief encounter came as no surprise. The cold night air brought relief from the heat inside. He got to his car, climbed into the driver's seat, and started the engine, noting with relief the left-over warmth of the car's interior. He put the car in reverse and backed into the center of the parking lot before pulling out of the driveway and onto the country road.

Cliff took advantage of Bruce Springsteen on the radio and turned up the volume to help clear his head. A half mile to the main road, and another quarter to the 7-Eleven. The convenience store lot was empty, except for an old pickup truck in the parking lot. Cliff pulled into a spot in front of the well-lit store and got out of the car.

As he turned the corner on the walkway and headed toward the automatic door, Cliff noticed a shape on the ground, lying close to the corner of the building. Not sure what it was, he approached with hesitation, before recognizing the shape of a person. A man in a navy pea-coat and knit wool hat, lying half on his back, half on his side, not moving.

Cliff's medical persona leaped into action, and he pounced to the ground beside the man, grabbing and shaking his upright shoulder, shouting, "Hey, buddy. Are you OK? Hey…" He checked. The man seemed not to be breathing. Cliff felt for a pulse in his neck. Nothing.

He saw no one else near the store and jumped to his feet. He ran to the door and yelled in, "Call 911! Call 911 right now!" Returning to the man's side, he checked again: still no breathing, no heart rate, setting into full gear the automatic Cliff.

He flipped the man on his back and lifted between his shoulder blades to tilt his chin up, his head back. Then he grabbed the stubbled jaw, pulled it forward with one hand, and pinched his nostrils with the other. Placing his lips against those of the unconscious man, he blew two full breaths into the man's lungs, grateful when he felt them fill with his own air.

He paused. There was no reaction and Cliff delivered a "precordial thump." Grasping both hands together, like a volleyball player trying to make a save, he raised them above his head and brought them down on the middle of the man's chest. Still nothing.

It was time to start chest compressions, and Cliff gave five. He had done this so many times, he could have done it in his sleep. He returned to give him another two breaths. This time he noticed the iciness of the man's lips, and he knew the cold was from more than the freezing night air.

Cliff knew the man was dead. He'd likely been dead for a while. But Cliff did not stop. Chest compressions, two, three, four … breath … chest compressions. He could not be sure how long this continued but it was long enough that his arms and lower back ached. Cliff was familiar with this routine enough to realize that the aches rarely became too much to bear. But then, CPR without the help of an entire team was something new. Ignoring the ache, he continued. And even with the freezing cold, sweat rolled down his sideburns.

At last, flashing red lights strobed the parking lot, followed by a lot of noise — banging truck doors, clanging metal, and then a stretcher on wheels pushed by two overweight paramedics. Cliff's relief was palpable when they ordered, "We'll take over." One placed a clear, soft plastic mask over the man's mouth and nose, and squeezed the bag which would give him breaths. The other continued the chest compressions begun by Cliff, who was suddenly aware of the sour taste in his mouth.

Cliff backed away a few feet to the edge of the walkway and watched as the paramedics continued their work. They exuded confidence and competence. With perfect coordination they lifted the man onto the collapsed gurney without ever missing a breath or a compression. A third attendant, the driver, now joined them, helping to raise the gurney and wheel it to the ambulance.

Cliff seemed to disappear into the darkness, though he had not moved from his spot on the sidewalk. No one spoke to him, and within minutes the back door of the truck slammed shut, a siren cried out, and the ambulance rushed back to the road. He continued to stand alone surrounded by the dark. The siren and the flashing lights both faded in the distance, and finally Cliff scuffed his way back to his car. The engine started with ease, and Cliff drove back in a slight daze, returning finally to his condo.

When he passed through the front door, Darlene stood there, looking angrier than before, Ryan screaming in her arms.

"Where the fuck have you been?" she screamed. And seeing his empty arms, "Where is the fuckin' milk?"

Cliff shrugged and turned toward the bathroom. But then he stopped and turned back toward Darlene, holding his arms out for Ryan. She handed the boy over and stomped down the short hall, slamming the door of the bedroom.

Cliff bounced Ryan gently in his arms, and his cries quieted, morphing into giggles. Cliff's fatigue began soon to descend on him also, like the dark shadow of a cloud passing overhead, and he sat on the couch, still cuddling the boy, whose nose was still dripping.

Ryan laid his head on Cliff's chest. His breathing soon became rhythmic, and Cliff pulled himself from his own drifting to see that Ryan had fallen asleep. Slowly and quietly, Cliff rose from the couch and carried Ryan to his room where he laid him in his crib.

After Ryan settled, Cliff once again turned toward the bathroom. He could not remember a shower seeming more inviting.

MUSIC 101

Karen's numb fingers fumbled with the key in the steel lock of the school door. As she exhaled, her breath was visible in the cold morning air. She was to arrive at the school, and the others probably wouldn't start showing up for another twenty minutes or so. These were the same stiff fingers that were nimble, the ones that had gotten her through the music program at Indiana University, and gotten her a master's degree. The same fingers that caressed her violin strings on their way to the second chair in the Toledo symphony.

The lock finally gave in to Karen's jiggling key in one hand, as she opened the door holding her small coffee thermos in the other. The school was dark. Outside, the February Saturday morning was gray. She flipped the switch to the hall light and made her way to the music room.

As she walked down the dim hallway, she wondered: was she crazy to take this project on? Why not be content with her orchestra appointment, and her teaching position at the university? What did she know about "at risk" children? The brochure promised the opportunity to "make a difference" in their lives. That was about all she knew.

To Karen, "at risk children" was only a phrase. Her father was a psychiatrist who taught and saw patients at the university hospital in Oregon. Her mother was an accomplished cellist who also taught in the music department at the same university. Karen and her brother were comfortable as children, and that comfort was part of the reason she had been eager to leave and begin her own journey several years ago. That journey took her through music studies and degrees in Indiana, and then the appointments in northwest Ohio.

After some thought, Karen decided to volunteer for the program. And, somehow, she was now not only in charge of the string portion of the program, but the supervisor for the program as a whole. She worried a bit that no one in her group was more qualified than she.

The "faculty" for the program were a motley crew. She was in charge of the strings. Lizard was teaching percussion. She knew from his application that he was the twenty-something drummer for a local rock band. Karen was puzzled. Though she didn't even know him yet, she could not help wondering what would motivate the barely-out-of-teens rock band drummer to spend his time with a bunch of poor, raucous kids. Or so she imagined them — raucous.

Karen knew the keyboardist personally. Alfred was the pianist for the symphony. He was well-thought of, and she had recruited him herself for this project. He agreed, but she thought it was mainly because they had gone out a few times. He seemed interested in her, and motivated. She hoped there was some motivation for the program as well.

Karen knew the man in charge of the choir responsibilities only by his reputation. He was the director of a locally-celebrated choir. The choir was more known for its open invitation to anyone wishing to sing than for the prominence of its performances, though they had something of a cult following. And the members seemed always happy. Randy, the director, she knew, also had a penchant for a more unusual than traditional repertoire. They practiced in his mid-town home, and the neighbors could hear the voices' crescendos from several houses down. They either enjoyed it, or they hated it.

This morning was a little more than a week before the start of the program, and this was the first meeting of those who would be its teachers. Mostly it would be a first-time introduction for all of them, as well, as they met to discuss plans for the coming weeks. From the résumés Karen had read, she guessed that none of them had much experience with underprivileged kids, and that made her nervous. There was a social worker, Margaret Sims, who was had overall charge of the program, and she would be available to help. Other than that, they would be pretty much on their own.

Karen purposely left the door unlocked, and before she could even arrange chairs for everyone in the music room, she heard the boiler-room clunk of the front door opening and closing.

"Hello!" she yelled, unsure who was the target of her greeting. A few footsteps, and then a man's voice, "Hello." A young man stood in the doorway, the top of his head nearly touching the door frame with a shag of robust, metallic green hair. Karen looked up. This must be Lizard, she thought.

"Hi. I'm Karen."

"Hi. I'm Leonard Kowalski. Pleased to meet you."

"Leonard?"

"Yeah. Most people call me Lizard, though." He held out his hand to shake in introduction. Karen took the hand and shook it vigorously.

"Well, I am glad to meet you. Welcome to the TEMP."

"The what?"

"Oh, sorry. They just decided on the name. The 'Toledo Experimental Music Program.' Like I said, I'm Karen. I am sort of in charge. I think." Lizard smiled, uncommittedly. Karen noticed that he too had a thermos, only his was larger and metal. She motioned for him to sit in one of the chairs she'd begun arranging around the only table in the room.

"Join me in a cup of coffee?"

"Good idea, ma'am." And he pulled a chair out from the table, dropped his backpack to the floor, and sat, scooting the chair back up to the table.

"So, how did you come to sign up for this project, Lizard?" Karen was truly curious.

"Well, I saw the poster on the bulletin board in Sam's Vinyl Emporium — I go there a lot — and I thought it might be something I would like to do."

"Yeah," Karen said. "It was pretty much the same with me. I didn't really know much about what I was getting into. And I still don't, for that matter."

"The students are from the poor parts of town, right?" Lizard raised his eyebrows while pouring steaming coffee from his thermos into its cup.

"That's what I was told. And I guess that is what caught my interest."

"Oh? How so?"

Just then they heard the door's resonant crash echoing through the hallway. They both looked up. Within seconds a man with short-cropped, pure white hair appeared in the doorway, his cheeks ruddy with the cold, a broad smile accentuating the sweeping, theatrical gesture of his arm.

"Bonjour, monsieur et mademoiselle. Randy DuChamps here, at your service, and primed for a musical extravaganza!"

"Hello," Karen and Lizard replied together.

Karen rose from her seat. "I am Karen. I am supposed to be in charge. Glad to meet you, Randy. I've heard a lot about you."

"Ah, yes. The tales of my antics have traveled far, and I'm proud of some, but not so much of others."

Lizard stood and held out his hand. "Leonard."

Karen corrected him. "He goes by Lizard." Randy and Lizard shook hands in an enthusiastic manly clasp. "The pleasure is all mine, Lizard."

Karen assumed a motherly, leader-like role. "Randy, Lizard and I just sat down to have a cup of coffee while we waited for the others. Care to join us? I've got plenty."

"I do too," Lizard piped in. "I'm sure we could find another cup around here." And he began searching the cabinets above a sink in the front of the room.

"Don't mind if I do," Randy replied with another sweeping gesture of his arm, and broad smile. He took a chair as Lizard returned with a mug with a Christmas tree on its side, and poured from his thermos, handing the cup to Randy.

"Randy, we've heard so much about you and your choir, and we're so glad you wanted to join us." Karen continued her gentle inquiry. "What prompted you to sign up?"

"Well, my dear Karen, let me tell you. I have always been one to believe in community strength. It is only in community that we individuals find strength. So, I've given my life to strengthening community. And when I heard about this program at one of the churches that sponsors my choir, I thought, 'This is made for me!' Or, maybe, 'I am made for this program!'"

Karen was saved from responding by the loud clunk of the door once again. "That must be Alfred." A tall man in a suit and trench coat appeared in the doorway. His graying dark, thick hair was covered by a Homburg hat with a small green feather sticking up from the thin trim band atop the brim. He looked at the three as he removed the hat, and said with a faint English accent, "Hello."

Karen greeted him as he unbuttoned his coat. "Hello, Alfred. Welcome. Randy and Lizard, this is Alfred. He is the pianist with the symphony, and he will be in charge of the keyboard portion of our program." The other two nodded in greeting, and Alfred, as he removed his coat, inquired, "Lizard?" raising his eyebrows slightly.

"That's what everyone calls him," Karen interjected.

"Yes. That's what everyone calls me, but you are welcome to call me Leonard if you prefer."

Alfred hung his overcoat on the coat hook next to the door. Taking a chair at the table, he looked at each of them. "Yes. Have we begun discussing our plans?"

Karen quickly chimed in, "Actually, no. We were just getting to know one another. We were waiting for you."

"Well, so here I am. Shall we get started?"

"Why, yes. Certainly." Karen began. "As you all know, we will be working with — I mean teaching — children who come from, shall we say, difficult circumstances. They have been screened and all identified as high risk. Whatever that means."

"That means they will likely be boorish and know nothing about music. And probably have no interest in learning." Alfred's accent seemed a bit more noticeable.

"Nonsense!" Randy retorted. "I never met a youngster I couldn't teach to sing like an opera star!"

Karen remained poised. "I guess in any case, we will have to be quite good teachers, right?"

Randy nodded and Alfred rolled his eyes.

41

"I'll have no difficulty with that," Alfred said.

"So we don't have a final count yet, but I was told we could expect about twenty kids," Karen continued. "They will all be between eight and ten years old."

"Do any of them have any experience with music in any form?" Randy asked.

"I'm not sure. I think we should assume not. Starting with a clean slate."

Lizard listened intently without speaking, sipping a bit noisily on his hot coffee. His eyes were attentively moving back and forth among the others as each spoke. Alfred was next.

"So, what exactly is the program, the plan? We've got violin, drums, piano and voice. How are we going to teach them all of that in twelve short weeks?"

"Well, first of all ..." Karen tried to muster an answer. "It is only twelve weeks, but it is three afternoons a week, and for two hours each day. So we will have some time at least to introduce them to the wonders that are possible with music. Right?"

Alfred frowned at the fingers of his folded hands. Lizard nodded slightly.

Karen continued. "We can structure this any way we want. The sponsors really don't know music or teaching. They just want to see us put together something that works and helps these kids. I thought perhaps we could start by having the entire group together, and we could each spend some time talking about the music we each like. What do you think?"

Randy replied he thought that was "marvelous." Alfred and Lizard said nothing, Lizard waiting for Karen to continue.

"I thought that might be something of an introduction. Give them a glimpse of the different forms music might take. Perhaps it would even give them an opportunity to be drawn to one musical expression or another.

And then, after that, I was thinking we could work with the group as a whole a bit more, but let them begin to experiment with the different forms we bring. Not force them all to do everything, but give them all an opportunity to try one or more or all of the things we bring while we are all still together. That would further their opportunity to be attracted to one form or another. Thoughts?"

"Superlative!" exclaimed Randy

"Sounds pretty good to me," said Lizard a bit quietly. Alfred continued staring at the fingers more accustomed to Beethoven's piano concertos than to being folded on a table.

"That might take more than one session, or class... or whatever we will call them," Karen concluded. "But soon after, perhaps different students will begin to gravitate toward one or another of the four of us, and what we bring to them."

Alfred finally spoke. "Do you think it is a good idea to restrict them, after their introduction, to just one form, rather than to let them roam from one form to another?"

"Good point," Lizard offered.

Karen frowned. "I guess we could start with that kind of introduction and then afterward, just see where it goes, and do what seems best. What do you think?"

"Stupendous, Karen. Absolutely stupendous." Randy beamed.

The conversation continued for another forty-five minutes, covering topics like seating arrangements, number and duration of break times, and whether or not to provide snacks.

Before they were finished and putting on their coats, hats and boots, they agreed that they were as ready as they were going to be, and D-Day was but eight days away. They had exchanged phone numbers and e-mail addresses, and promised that they would contact the others with additional questions, suggestions, or panic-attacks. Each would also prepare some preliminary ideas for the first introductory sessions, and they would all share these ideas by e-mail.

After everyone had moved out the door of the school, Karen staying behind to fight once again with the ancient, frozen deadbolt, Alfred sidled up to her.

"Where are you headed? Care for a proper cup of coffee in a *real* coffee shop? And maybe we could hang at your place, or mine, for a bit after?"

***

Karen had a routine. Every morning, her clock radio would intone the news, or the weather, or if she were lucky, some nice piece of music advertising an upcoming local performance.

Once she was awake, which sometimes took fifteen or more minutes of listening to the drone of radio news voices, she would peel the covers and duvet from her naked shoulders, and roll toward the side of the bed, where she knew her running garb was folded on the awaiting chair, the running shorts and shirt. Except at this time of year, they were joined by long johns and a fleece-lined sweatshirt. After the socks and running shoes, she would be out the door by 6 a.m. Her morning three-mile run took her down Islington, and then Collingwood — mostly commercial streets, with true neighborhoods interlaced. This early Monday morning was much like all the others.

Karen's was a one-bedroom apartment, laid out "shotgun" style, narrow, and moving straight from front to back — living room, kitchen, bathroom, then bedroom. Sparse. Last night's dishes still filled the sink. She thought of that as she scuffed her way to the bathroom.

There was time to brush her teeth, but knowing that the first step in a run was the worst, she wasted no time. Locking her apartment door, she wound her way downstairs to the mammoth front entrance, which guarded the entire building. She pushed the door open, stepped into the frigid air, and launched into her run.

The sidewalks were made narrow by the foothills of snow pushed aside by plows overnight, but they were mostly clean and not slippery. And Karen was able to stride into her reverie. She heard music, magnificent violin concerti. And she thought about things usually forgotten. Her mom and dad. Her little brother, with his ambition to be recruited as a quarterback from his small Oregon town high school to a major university.

She thought about her dog that she'd left behind. Sloopy. No, not Snoopy. Sloopy, after that goofy old song her dad played now and again, "Hang On Sloopy ..." Yes, that was her dog, the rescued-from-the-pound, German Shepherdish mix, who loved her more than even her parents did.

I left Sloopy behind? And now, as her breath was becoming colder and her legs starting to complain, she wondered, *Why did I leave? Why did I leave Sloopy alone?*

When her three-mile, half-hour run was finished, Karen returned home sweaty and warmer than might be expected, given the early morning single-digit temperature. She was eager for the shower, and luxuriated in its warm, skin-stroking fingertips on her shoulders and back. After a quick dry and dress for the day, it was time for her yogurt/granola/fruit cup. She sat at her kitchen counter, savoring the blueberries and raspberries, then quickly grabbed her things for the orchestra rehearsal. She was nervous. The first kids' class was tonight.

Rehearsal went well. The orchestra's concert was only three weeks away, and they were featuring Bach's Concerto in D-Minor for Two Violins, a formidable choice for the entire orchestra, but especially for Karen. Alfred made the piano part look easy, but Karen was still struggling with her part of the violin duet.

After rehearsal, while the orchestra members gathered their instruments, overcoats, hats and gloves, Alfred sauntered over to the string section. "Care for a bit of lunch?"

Karen looked up from her violin case. "I don't think so, Alfred. I have some things to do before our first class for the kids this afternoon."

"Oh, yes. I had forgotten all about that."

"But you are coming, aren't you?" Karen gasped.

Alfred ogled Karen's blouse, and then her jeans. "If you are going to be there, so will I."

"Good, then. I will see you later at the school." She closed the violin case, stood up, wrapped her scarf around her neck, and put her coat on before heading out the door.

She arrived at the high school just before 3:00. Students were just finishing classes, and were heading from their lockers to the doors, or in some cases to one or another room for Chess or Debate Club, the Yearbook Club, or to the gym for basketball practice. Karen marched directly to the band room, where the last student musicians were just leaving. Behind her, two men from the maintenance crew wheeled a large cart stacked with a number of boxes into the room.

"Are you Miss Karen? These are some things that arrived at the shipping dock for you."

"Oh, thank you so much. Those must be the instruments for the kids."

"You're welcome ma'am. You have a good evening."

They were to receive student instruments from the Catholic Board of Education for their use in the TEMP program. A half-dozen portable keyboards and an equal number of student violins. A larger box contained a variety of percussion instruments. Karen dived into the packages, opening them one at a time. She would have to check the tuning of the strings. She could help the kids learn how to do that later. With only an hour before they were to arrive, she set about her work.

"Karen?" She looked up and saw a portly middle-aged woman with her gray hair bound back in a bun. It was Mrs. Sims, the social worker. "Hi. I am glad that your equipment arrived on time."

"Yes, Margaret. None too early, I might add."

"I must speak with you about one of the children, Latisha. She is nine years old, and she comes from a very rough family. No father. One older brother, and a younger brother and sister."

"Sounds like it could be any of the kids, doesn't it?"

"Well. Latisha, I am told by the principal at her school, is having extra difficult problems. Her mother had a drug problem, and about two months ago, she OD'd. Her kids found her on their living room couch the next morning, not moving or breathing. Apparently, she'd already been dead for a while."

"Oh my God!" Karen covered her mouth

"Latisha and her younger sister moved in with their grandmother, who isn't in such good health herself. And the boys have been placed in foster care. Ever since all of this happened, Latisha has been very, very angry. She's been throwing things, breaking things, hitting other kids. She's had to be removed from class nearly a dozen times, and her principal says she is going to have to expel her if this continues. I just wanted you to know. Please tell me if there are any problems."

"Thanks, Margaret. Oh. That poor girl."

"Your heart may not be so forgiving and empathetic if her behavior is anything like it's been described!

You call me if you have any problems."

As Mrs. Sims turned to leave, Lizard walked in behind her.

"Hi, Karen. I see everything got here, just in time."

"Yes. I was getting a little worried. All of your stuff is in the big box on the end."

Lizard responded, "Thanks," and he started removing the contents from the box: several tambourines, maracas, shakers, wood blocks, drumsticks, wooden spoons, and — at the very bottom — a single electronic drum pad.

"Wow!" Lizard looked like a kid on Christmas morning.

Meanwhile, Karen finished unpacking the violins and had begun checking their tuning. She was surprised that they needed very little, only a bit of adjustment here and there. Alfred appeared at the door, removing his overcoat. He was dressed more casually than usual in an Italian silk shirt and designer jeans. He pulled off his ankle-high galoshes to reveal perfectly polished leather loafers.

"Salutations and good eventide to my fellow faculty and friends!" Randy appeared from nowhere, eyes sparkling and ruddy cheeks broadly smiling. "How is everyone this fine day?"

"Great, Randy. We're opening up the boxes of instruments we will be using. I guess your only box is your voice box, so you're off the hook," Karen said.

"We have a sign-in/attendance sheet on the table for the kids when they start to arrive. And name-tags and marker for them to write their names. We should also wear name-tags, I think. And when the kids start to arrive, they won't all come at the same time. So, I was thinking that one of us should meet each one, introduce ourselves, and start getting to know each other. As others arrive, they will be added to the small groups forming, so that when all are here, we will each have a small group of about five kids. Does that sound okay?"

"Yeah."

"Sure."

"Splendid. Perfect."

Karen continued. "I am a little nervous. Is anyone else?"

Randy laughed. "Poppycock. Why would I be nervous about teaching children to sing? I've been doing that all my life!"

"Nervous?" grunted Alfred, with a sarcastic snicker.

They could barely hear Lizard's voice. "Yeah. I guess I am. A little ... But at least they gave us some pretty cool percussion stuff."

It was about five minutes to four when the first child appeared at the door. Signs had been posted in the hallway directing the children and their parents, or whoever brought them, to the band room. Karen thought she might as well take this boy on.

"Hi. My name is Karen. What's yours?" The boy's eyes went to the floor and she could barely hear his voice.

"Malik," he answered without lifting his eyes. Karen held out her hand. "Glad to meet you, Malik." He placed his half-opened hand tentatively in hers.

Two girls walked in, and were greeted first by Randy, and then by Lizard. Each adult pulled a couple of chairs into different corners and began to chat with their chosen child. Alfred was inspecting the keyboards.

For another fifteen minutes the kids straggled into the band room. Only a few were accompanied by an adult. Karen guessed that most had been left off at the front door. But the room was filled with a soft background noise of children's chatter, punctuated now and then by a loud laugh or catcall. It was 4:15, and she counted the children. Nineteen. Margaret had confirmed that twenty children were registered, so someone was missing.

Karen wound her way to the front of the room, faced the children and their "mentors," and cleared her throat. "Hello, children. For those I haven't met yet, my name is Karen, and I will be helping each of you enjoy our music program for the next few weeks. My colleagues are Alfred," indicating him with a nod of her head and gesture of her hand. "Alfred is a pianist. A piano player.

"This is Randy, who teaches singing." Randy rose to his feet, and bent forward in a formal bow, like a beau greeting his partner on a parlor dance floor. Two or three of the kids had difficulty stifling giggles.

"And the young man with the green hair is *not* from Mars. He is Lizard, the drummer from the band Agent Orange." The kids all laughed and clapped, and Lizard looked down, embarrassed.

One of the boys, African-American — about ¾ of the children were — spoke up. "How tall are you?"

"Six-five."

"Man, you shoulda been a basketball player, not no drummer!"

Lizard smiled.

Karen explained the plan. Randy would first introduce them into group vocal exercises. The chairs were regrouped into a semicircle facing the front of the room, where Randy quickly took his place.

"Ladies and gentlemen... It is my great pleasure this evening to introduce you to 'rounds.' What is that, you may ask. Well, let me tell you...

Rounds is a type of music where different people, or groups of people, sing the same thing, but starting at different times. The song we are going to sing in rounds is a very old one, but one that lots of people know. It's called, 'Make New Friends.' So, we will spend the next half-hour or so learning the melody and the words which I have written out. Karen, would you pass around the hand-outs?"

Karen had no idea that Randy would be so well prepared. Everything seemed so well thought out. And he made hand-outs? She found the short stack of papers, and handed them to the first student in the front row.

"Let me sing the first four lines for you, and then you can sing them with me:
*Make new friends,
but keep the old.
One is silver,
the other gold."*

Randy's voice boomed making the band room suddenly seem smaller. The kids sat in their chairs, eyes wide open, and mouths, too. Randy was remarkable!

"Okay. Now I will sing one line, and I will stop. That's when I want you to pick up and sing the same line. Okay?"

The next half-hour became forty-five minutes, and it went by like it was barely ten. The children were captured. By the end of Randy's time, they'd mastered the first verse, and he had them try once to do it in a two-part rounds. They ended up laughing.

It was time for a break. Karen had brought fruit juices, and she opened the cooler, handing out the cellophane-wrapped boxes one by one. Randy had dried out their vocal cords, she thought.

Karen called them together again after fifteen minutes. "We are halfway through our class. Or, our fun session. I like that better. So next I'd like to introduce you again to our non-Martian. Lizard is going to show us the wonder of drums, and tambourines, and... pots and pans, and anything else you can bang on." The kids clapped at once.

Lizard came up to the front of the room. "The first thing we are going to do is learn how to make a beat. But you already know that." A couple of the kids looked puzzled, but Lizard continued.

"We are going to start really simple. Everyone is going to get a drumstick. We have enough. Also, everyone is going to get something else: some will get a tom-tom drum and drumstick, some will get a tambourine. Some won't get anything, so you will have to find something nearby to bang on. Then, I am going to play you a CD. Okay? Karen, would you pass out the instruments please."

Soon they all had their instruments and were looking wide-eyed into Lizard's eyes.

"First, we are going to count. We are all going to count together."

The children looked around at each other, puzzled.

"Let's start by counting to four. After we hit four, we start over again. Ready?" And he began, "One, two, three, four. One, two, three, four. Come on now, everyone." And one by one, the children began to join in, "One, two, three, four."

Lizard halted their chorus. "Stop. Now were are going to try something else. This time, we are going to count to four, but instead of saying 'four,' we will each make a sound instead. Like this." And he began, holding a tambourine, "One, two, three," and he hit the tambourine. Then he repeated the same sequence.

"Each of you has an instrument, right?" Two of the children raised empty hands, and Lizard spoke to them. "That's okay. We have something special for you." He smiled at the empty-handed boy and girl. "Everyone else must make a noise with your instrument instead of saying four. I want you drummers to hit your drum two times instead of saying four. And you with tambourines, I want you to hit your tambourine, like this, two times also." Got it?

The two children without instruments looked disappointed. Lizard looked at them. "Ah, my friends. Don't look so sad. You are going to do something different from everyone else. You will clap your hands instead of saying four. But not twice. You will clap quickly three times, just like this. One, two, three," clap-clap-clap. "Okay everyone got it. Ready? Let's go. One, two, three," and suddenly there was an uncertain cacophony of noise.

"Good!" Lizard said. "That was great!" Now, let's try doing the same thing, only repeating it several times." And again the counting began. Each time they reached the dropped four, the sounds of drums and tambourines and triple claps became more coordinated. And the children were laughing. They were having fun.

Suddenly there appeared in the doorway of the band room a girl, like a black banshee, hair nappy and unkempt, still wrapped in a well-worn, down-filled Walmart coat and mittened hands.

"Is there a Miss Karen here?"

Karen rose from her chair. "I am Karen. And who are you?"

"Latisha."

"Oh." Karen paused, surprised. "Well... I am... I mean, we are really glad you made it, Latisha. Come in. We are nearly finishing here, but you are welcome for the rest of the time we have.

"This young man is Lizard. He is our drummer. He is teaching us about rhythm. If you'd like, you can have a seat and join us."

"Whatever," the girl snarled. She pulled her mittens off, and then removed her coat before taking a seat at the periphery of the group.

Lizard picked up where he'd left off. "Let's try this one more time, for just one more minute. Ready?" The kids were slightly distracted by the newcomer, and the promise of coordination in their drumming regressed.

Lizard addressed the kids. "Next time, we are going to learn some other, different rhythms. Okay?" The kids all nodded.

Karen moved to the front. "It's nearly six, so it's time to put away the things we've used. Please bring your things up to the front and put them onto the table. And we will see you tomorrow. I don't know about you, but I have had so much fun, I can hardly wait."

A few of the kids clapped, as they all rose and brought their items to the front table.

"This sucks!"

The room went silent, and everyone turned to Latisha, who still sat in her chair. "This whole thing sucks. It's a bunch of shit."

Karen tried to regain her poise. "Kids, please bring your things up to the front and get ready to start home. Latisha, if you'd like to talk, we can talk privately afterward."

Latisha snarled like an angry cornered cur. The other kids continued to bring their papers and instruments to the front table, while others began wrapping themselves in coats, acrylic caps, and gloves. One by one they left the classroom and wandered down the hall to their waiting parents, siblings, or other caregivers. Latisha sat, glowering into the empty space before her. She hadn't begun to don her winter coat.

Lizard, Alfred and Randy were all gathering together their supplies, and replacing them in boxes.

"Where do these go?" Alfred asked.

"In the boxes and then into the closet there in the corner," Karen answered.

"Mais, oui, madame," Randy flourished.

Latisha still sat in her seat, like black barnacle on a dock, unmoving and silent.

While the guys moved the boxes into the corner closet, Karen moved toward Latisha, and pulled up a chair next to hers. "Latisha, what do you want to get from coming to this program?"

"Nothin.' I don't want shit. My grandmamma said I had to come, so I came."

"Do you think you might have fun here?"

"It sucks. What kind of fun can you have here?"

Karen was baffled, unsure what to say. "I have fun here," she said finally. "And I think some of the other kids do, too. Of course, this is just our first night, so there's lots to learn. And, hopefully, a lot more fun to be had."

Latisha sat, sullen-faced, saying nothing.

"Well, is your grandmother coming to pick you up?" Karen asked. "Perhaps I could walk you to the front. What do you say?"

"*No*! I can walk by myself!"

Karen was taken aback. "Okay. Let me know if I can help. And I hope we see you tomorrow — on time. We'd love to have you be part of our group."

Latisha rose and pulled on her coat, hat and gloves. Then she stomped to the door.

"Bye." Karen felt somehow bad, empty, and she didn't know why.

The guys had finished putting all their gear into the closet, and Randy and Lizard were putting on their coats. Alfred, coat in hand, approached Karen and asked, "Care for a drink?"

"I sure need one after tonight, but I think I'll pass."

"Too bad. Don't know what you're missing."

That night, Karen dreamed. She was hiking in the foothills of some towering mountains. Snow was about 8 inches deep. She was wearing high boots which kept her feet dry and relatively warm. Not sure where she was going, she followed the narrowing trail up. Winding her way through the snow-laden pines, she heard a rustling. Not sure what was making the sound, she carefully stepped from the trail into the deeper, packed snow. She move forward ten or so feet, and she heard the noise again, this time with an accompanying whimper, like that of a newborn baby.

Behind a tree Karen saw a small red fox, with its rear right foot caught in the teeth of a spring trap. It scuffled, trying to pull its leg free, but there was no loosening. In her dream, Karen quietly approached the terrified animal, and she bent forward to open the lips of the trap. As she did, the fox pulled its leg free, and turned and sank its teeth into her gloved hand before running off.

Karen didn't remember the dream until the next morning, when she was brushing her teeth, and getting ready for her morning run. When the dream came suddenly back to her, her face framed by the bathroom mirror, toothbrush protruding from her mouth, she suddenly stopped brushing. And a feeling of sadness enshrouded her.

As she pushed closed the heavy wooden door of the apartment building, again feeling the cold slap of the February air, her legs felt heavier. And as she began her run, her stride seemed different — more off-balance, slower. It was not one of her better runs.

This morning was another orchestra rehearsal, and later, a violin lesson with a young girl. Karen had a few private students, and their tuition helped with her expenses. The Toledo Symphony was not known for its generosity. And then, there was the TEMP class this evening. Not a terrible day ahead, but a pall hung over her. The dream? Anxiety about the TEMP session? Karen wasn't sure, but her morning run was far from her best.

Karen finished her fruit cup, bundled up and headed out the door. Rehearsal went well. She noticed Alfred avoided her afterward. She headed home to warmth, a cup of tea, and some thinking about the TEMP kids. Especially Latisha. She recalled the exchanges of the evening before. Latisha was so angry. She could ruin everything for all the others. But Karen still felt drawn to her, as though by some paranormal spell.

Three o'clock came more quickly than it seemed it should have, and Karen again headed out into the winter air to walk toward Central Catholic. It was close, and she arrived in less than fifteen minutes. The door was open, and high schoolers were exiting and entering, lingering. She made her way to the band room.

Once there, she again reordered the room, scooting the folding metal chairs into three semicircular rows, forming a sort of theater, or amphitheater effect. She pulled the boxes from the corner closet, and first looked for her violins. Tonight they would introduce strings and keyboards to the kids, so it was Karen's night. And Alfred's.

Randy arrived, followed soon by Lizard.

"Hi, guys!"

The two men muttered hello, with Randy removing his English touring cap with a flourish.

"Are you all set for Day 2?" Karen asked.

"As ready and steady as can be," said Randy. "I am most curious to see if the young girl from last night shows up again. She was a piece of work, indeed!"

"Randy, I wouldn't call her a 'piece of work.' She has been through a lot. She will probably be a challenge for us, but I am not sure it is her fault at all. We should try to be really patient with her."

"Oh, yes. I didn't mean we shouldn't try to reach out to her." Randy for the first time, perhaps ever, looked a bit unnerved. Lizard merely watched the two conversing, taking it all in.

"Thanks, guys. I need all the help I can get. I mean, Latisha needs all the help we can give her."

Alfred rushed in the door. "Sorry. I'm a bit late, and I meant to be here early to set up the keyboards we have."

"*Pas de problème*, Alfred." Randy was gracious.

"What about that girl? The one who came in late. What was her name? What are we going to do with her?" Alfred seemed truly troubled.

"Yes," Randy said. "We were just discussing her."

"She is not 'that girl.' Her name is Latisha," said Karen. "And we are going to welcome her to our group and try to make her as comfortable as we can. Mrs. Sims told me about Latisha, and some of the problems she has been through in the last few months. Believe me: she is in the middle of a very difficult time. And anything we can do to help her will be a big plus."

"But... her language!" Randy protested. "Surely we cannot allow such language among all the other kids."

Malik shuffled through the door, eyes cast downward.

"Hello," he said to Karen.

"Hello, Malik. Are you ready to fiddle today?"

"Yes, ma'am." He took his seat in the front row. And soon the other children drifted in, one by one. Karen knew some of them by name, but most she did not. It was frustrating to say "hello" without having a name to attach.

The chairs were soon all filled. But the one Karen had been sure to watch was still empty. Latisha was not there.

Karen took her position at the front of the room. "Hello!" she said in an enthusiastic voice.

"Hello!" the children responded in a chorus that would have made Randy proud.

"What do you want to do today?" The kids collectively mumbled in what sounded like a low hum.

"You wanna make some music?" Karen was starting to feel like a cheerleader, and the kids erupted into a "Yeah!"

"Okay, then. Alfred is going to show you some keyboard tricks. Are you ready?"

"Yeah!"

Alfred sauntered to the front. He was still wearing the suit he'd worn to the rehearsal that morning. But his shirt was wrinkled, and his tie loosened and askew.

"Good afternoon, children. I am here with the hope of sharing with you today some of the secrets of the keyboard. This is how we will proceed. Here in the front, we have a grand piano. This is a _real_ piano. We also have six digital keyboards, which we will share with any of you who wish to learn more about the piano. But first, we will learn some simple duets together on the grand piano. Do you know what a duet is?"

The kids looked blankly at him. A few shook their heads.

"A duet is a piano piece for two people to play together. Some are very easy, but also very pretty. Which makes them perfect tunes for beginners to learn. Have you ever heard "Chopsticks?" A few nodded, but most shook their heads.

"First, I'd like to take a survey. How many of you are most interested in singing?" Four or five raised their hands. "And how many in drumming?" Another four or five.

"I know you haven't had a chance to hear or play the violin yet, but are any interested in the violin?" No one moved.

"Well, then. Finally, how many are interested in the piano, or the keyboard?" Three children raised their hands.

"Fine. I will need a few helpers to assist me demonstrating duets, so you three will be my assistants. If anyone else finds their interest growing, you too could join us later. But for now, let us begin with the very simple duet tune that has come to be known as 'Chopsticks.' I need my first assistant."

One of the boys in the front row waved his small black hand.

"You. What is your name, young man?"

"Jaylon."

"Well, Jaylon, please come up here to the piano with me and let's learn 'Chopsticks.' All the rest of you, you may leave your seats and come up and join us. Form a circle around the piano bench so you can see better what Jaylon is doing."

Alfred proceeded to show Jaylon how to hold his fingers, press the keys, at first just one at a time. And then he showed the boy how to play two and three keys at a time to make simple chords. He was teaching him the bass portion of "Chopsticks." Jaylon frowned intensely as he watched his own fingers. Alfred practiced just the bass part a dozen times. And, aware of the time, he invited the second of the children who were his "keyboard assistants."

"What is your name?"

"Alisha," the timid black girl responded.

"Alisha, please come up her and sit next to me, like Jaylon was. I want you to try this, too."

And so the lesson began anew. Alisha mastered the fingering, and rudimentary chords in just fifteen minutes. Alfred stood up from the piano and looked mostly at the piano "assistants," but also glanced out to the other kids.

"Our time is up. Next time we will break out the keyboards, and everybody who wants to will be able to try to play some of the things we've played tonight."

Just as Alfred was finishing his closing remarks, Latisha appeared like a large black beast in the doorway. She removed her coat and threw it to the floor, and found her own seat, toward the back of the circle. No one said anything, and the room seemed too quiet.

Karen jumped to the front of the room, and took over.

"Alfred, thank you so much for your introduction to the piano and the keyboard. I am very excited to see what is coming for all of us with piano and keyboard.

"My turn has come. We are going to try to see what it feels like to hold a violin. And then maybe a little bit, how to use to bow to make the violin start to sing. No songs or tunes tonight. Just getting to know the violin.

We have six violins we can use. I noticed no one raised their hand when we asked you who wanted to learn more about this instrument. So I am asking for volunteers. All those who raised your hand — oops, none of you. Ah... Okay... Would anyone be interested in meeting a violin for the first time?"

Four children raised their hands. And the first, from the back of the room, was Latisha. Karen's eyes widened in surprise, but just for a moment.

"Great! That's four of us. Would the four of you come up to the front and take chairs up here?" And the three moved forward, pushing aside backpacks and other items from the aisles. Karen pulled together four chairs, and arranged them in a semicircle that opened to the rest of the class. There were three girls, including Latisha, and a boy.

"Come up here and take a seat, and you will get your violin." Latisha took the seat on the far left.

"Lizard, will you hand out the instruments?" And Lizard rose and went to the lineup of violins Karen had assembled on the front desk. He took two, one in each hand, and approached the children, handing the instruments to the first two in the row. And then he took the two remaining violins to the two remaining children, lastly distributing the four bows.

Karen pointed to the parts of the violins, using her own as an example, while the children examined the corresponding parts on their own instruments.

"As you can see, there are four strings. This is called the fingerboard. Can anyone think of why it is called that?" The children's faces were without expression. Unperturbed, she continued.

"When you press your finger on the string, and press it against the fingerboard, you and the violin will make a sound when you draw the bow across it." She demonstrated several notes, some straight, some with vibrato.

"That sucks." Latisha scowled. "Sounds like a cat when you yank its tail real hard."

Karen looked at Latisha and quickly looked at the other three children. "Why don't we all try to make a sound? This is how you hold the violin, just like I was. On your shoulder, and under your chin. And watch. This is how you hold the bow in your fingertips, between your fingers and thumb. Try just holding the violin and the bow and pretend you are about to play a note."

The children grappled with their small instruments, finally getting them positioned beneath their chins, the bow in the other hand. Latisha struggled with hers, and was the last to get it in position.

"Now, don't press on the strings like I was, but just draw the bow across the large string on the top." Three of the violins moaned in agony. Latisha struggled holding the instrument and bow at the same time.

"Latisha, tuck the violin closer under your chin, like this."

Latisha twisted the violin on her shoulder, cocking her head, holding the delicate instrument like a slugger gripping a baseball bat.

"No, Latisha. Relax. More gently. Like this."

The girl raised the violin above her head and brought it crashing to the floor in front of her chair. "This is stupid! I hate this!"

Karen unconsciously pushed her chair back a foot, while the violin splintered before her. All she could think of was a rock star in concert, except that she was also frightened.

"Young lady!" Alfred jumped to his feet. "Just what do you think you are doing? You can't destroy property like that!"

"Oh yea, Whitey? Says who?"

"Says me, young lady," Alfred replied, undaunted.

"I ain't no young lady. Don't you call me that, you whitey asshole." She was on her feet. Randy and Lizard watched, wide-eyed.

Karen regathered her wits. "Okay, children. I think we are finished for tonight." The two hours were nearly up. "Let's all get our coats on. We'll see you all tomorrow night. Be careful out there."

The children bundled up in their mostly tattered winter coats, gloves, caps and boots, and began to file slowly out the door. Latisha moved to get her jacket, and kicked the splintered violin that was still on the floor in front of her chair. Without a look back, she stormed out the door, muttering "Whitey bitch!" under her breath.

Randy and Lizard began gathering the instruments and silently putting them back in their boxes, while Alfred, seething, moved the chairs back to their original places. Karen slumped back into her chair, sighing loudly enough to be heard by the others. She was still sitting, unmoving, when the others finished re-arranging the room. No one took their coats, and they stood awkwardly while she gazed into some faraway distance. No one spoke.

Without warning, Karen began to sob. Lizard watched from behind at her silhouette, slumped in the folding metal chair, while her shoulders began to bob silently, her forehead in her hands.

Alfred took a step back. "There, there. No need to cry, Karen."

"Oh, my." Randy looked almost nervous. "I don't think it is all that bad, Karen. Latisha is just a bad girl. There may be nothing we can do for her."

The room was filled with quiet, except for the near-silent sobs, and no one moved for a long while. Karen still sat, and behind her, Lizard. Finally, Alfred went to the coat hooks and carefully took down his coat. Randy looked confusedly from Karen to Alfred, and finally he too began to move toward the coat hooks, while Karen sat, no longer sobbing, but not moving.

Alfred was carefully dressed now for the cold, and began moving toward the door. "I guess I will see you all next time.

All except for that Latisha. I will not have her in this class ever again." Alfred's voice shook slightly, then softened. "Karen, will you be all right?"

She nodded. And Randy started to put on his coat as well. "Good night, Karen." He paused at the door and turned back to Karen. "Do you want to talk about what just happened?"

Karen was silent.

"Well. I am sure tomorrow will be a better day." His grin returned broadly. "Tomorrow will be a splendid day. Have a good night."

Randy and Alfred walked into the dark hallway. Lizard still stood awkwardly behind Karen, who was still silent, unmoving. After several minutes, he approached her, pulled a metal folding chair alongside hers, and sat, saying nothing.

They sat together, three, maybe four minutes, saying nothing, the dimmed classroom lights reflecting dimly from Lizard's metallic green hair. He reached over and placed his hand on Karen's shoulder. Her eyes still sparkled with diminishing tears. "Let's go home," she whispered.

"Yea. I got a gig at Tony Packo's in an hour. You okay?"

"I'll be okay. Sorry I got upset."

"No problem, Karen. It's cool."

Together they got up and got their winter garb. Karen fumbled in her coat pocket for the key to the front door, and they turned out the classroom lights, moving to the darkened hallway.

***

The sound of the alarm was like the distant, guttural hum of a caravan of 18-wheelers, or dozens of bikers pulling at once into a truck stop. Karen turned on her side, and hit the snooze button. She felt like she did back in school, when she'd stayed up all night, sleepless, practicing for a recital, her final exam the next morning. Pictures of Latisha smashing her violin flashed before her half-awake eyes. She turned back to her right, and soon fell again into troubled sleep.

It was so late when she awoke again that she had no time for her morning run, and barely time to dress and make it to rehearsal. She played her part of the Bach violin concerto, but her heart and mind were elsewhere. The whole orchestra seemed to pick up on her mood, she thought, and the entire practice seemed lethargic. Still, she was surprised when the time came to pack up the instruments. She placed her violin and bow into the velvet case. She took note that Alfred was not to be seen, apparently having left the hall immediately.

At home in her apartment, Karen fixed a tuna sandwich and glass of milk. Sitting at her kitchen table, she again opened her violin case, and carefully removed the instrument. Placing her sandwich aside, she began playing her part of the violin duet. It sounded so completely different without the other violin and the accompanying orchestra. It was mournful. She'd never noticed that before.

At three o'clock, another of her violin students rang at the outside door. Karen rose, and walked down the hallway stairs to unlock the door, and let the girl in. The girl was the daughter of a well-known pediatrician in town, and her mother was a teacher in the Catholic grade school a few blocks over. The girl was competent on the violin, but no prodigy.

When the end of the lesson arrived, and the girl was putting on her coat, Karen turned to her. "Julia, do you like the violin, taking lessons and all?"

"It's okay," she replied.

"Why are you taking lessons?"

Julia frowned. "Well, mostly because my mother wants me to, I guess."

Karen put on her own coat and escorted the young girl to the front door, and walked with her to the sidewalk before the two turned in opposite directions, the girl headed home, Karen to the video store to rent a movie for the evening.

The next morning, Karen managed to stay awake after her alarm sounded, and to complete her morning run before leaving for orchestra practice. As she pulled the heavy door to her apartment building closed, she felt a lump in her throat, and she wondered if she was coming down with a strep infection. But she knew that wasn't it.

Practice seemed better than it had the day before, and once

again she did not see Alfred afterward. After practice she again headed home, and practiced her violin part some more before leaving for the TEMP class. When she got to the school's band room, she found that she was not the first to arrive, as she usually was. Walking into the room, she found Lizard was already arranging the chairs and removing instruments from the boxes.

"You're early, Lizard. How was your gig the other night?"

"Good. It was good. There was a pretty good crowd, and we seemed like we were in a bit of a zone. It was fun. Oh, I thought I'd come a bit early and help you set up."

"Oh, thank you, Lizard. That's really nice of you."

Lizard looked at her somewhat quizzically. "Are you okay, Karen? I was a little worried about you the other night."

"Oh, I'm fine, Lizard. Really. Well... maybe not fine, but a lot better than I was Tuesday."

"Good. I'm glad." He paused briefly, then continued. "I think how you're trying to help that girl is really good."

"Thanks, Lizard. I just feel very bad for her. You can't imagine what all she's been through. I just don't know how to reach her, though."

"I bet you'll figure something out, Karen."

Just then Randy burst through the door, sweeping from his head a maroon beret, flourishing it in a grand gesture. "Oh my, oh my! The sunshine today! Spring must be soon approaching." Randy had a way to make Karen chuckle, no matter what her mood.

Two of the children came running squealing into the room, then slowed as soon as they got inside.

"Hello, Miss Karen," they said together. "We're early."

Alfred walked in behind them. He looked at the already-arranged room and the instruments already set out on the table. "Well. I see somebody has been busy getting ready."

"We didn't want to waste any time getting back to your piano duets," Karen said.

More of the children came in, chattering and removing their outerwear, then taking seats. Latisha was not among them.

Karen moved to the front of the room. "Hi, kids. Did everyone have a good day off yesterday?"

"Yeah!"

"Anybody practice your music?" The room fell silent.

"Anybody *listen* to some music?"

"Yeah!"

"Oh, good. What did you listen to?"

One of the girls in front waved her hand in excitement. "Yes, Adalia? What did you listen to?"

"Beyonce," she said with a wide grin.

Karen looked at the other kids. Malik stared at the floor. "What about you, Malik? Did you listen to some music?"

"Yes, ma'am."

"So what did you listen to?" She expected Kanye West, or 50 Cent.

"B.B. King, ma'am."

"He's good, isn't he, Malik?"

"Yes ma'am."

"So who would like to start making some music of our own?"

They cheered, "Yeah!"

"Let's start back with the piano. Alfred, would you begin?"

"Yes, indeed. May I have my three assistants with me again, please? And the rest of you come up and gather around the piano like we did the last time."

Karen glanced toward the door.

Alfred started by reviewing the bass portion of "Chopsticks" they had learned during the last class. Each of the three "assistants" took a turn practicing. Then Alfred announced that he was going to play along with each of them at the same time. When Jaylon returned to the bench and started playing his bass parts, Alfred began the treble portion. It took some time to coordinate, which was never quite accomplished, before it was time for the other two "assistants" to try.

When Alfred's hour was up, Karen went to the front again, and asked as the pianists were returning to their seats, "Who wants some fruit juice?"

"Yeah!" And Karen removed the juice boxes from the cooler.

When the short break was over, Karen glanced again at the empty door. Then, "Lizard, I think we are all ready for some more percussion. I will hand out the instruments."

Lizard began with a brief instruction about different beats, explaining that the fourth beat — with the drumsticks and tambourines — was a "backbeat."

"And now we're going to do the same thing with the second beat. On the count of two, I want all the tambourine players to hit their tambourine two times quickly. And on the count of four, I want the drummers to hit their drums twice quickly and the clappers to clap three times."

Karen frowned, wondering if the children could follow instructions that partly baffled even her. They seemed to catch on quickly, however, and the second hour was soon over. Karen again came forward.

"Okay, kids. For your homework tomorrow and over the weekend, I want everyone to spend 15 minutes listening to music every day — your stereo, your iPod, whatever. And I'd like you to pick out your favorite music to listen to — rap or hip-hop, jazz, blues, gospel... whatever you like. And then on Monday, let's talk about what we listened to and tell each other why we chose what we did." She glanced again at the door. "Did everyone have fun?"

"Yeah!"

And almost as one, they rushed the coat hooks and prepared to leave. As the last child walked out the door, Karen again glanced over, while the guys began putting the room and instruments back in order. Alfred and Randy both excused themselves early as both said they had other commitments, leaving Karen and Lizard to finish the cleanup.

"Karen, why don't you leave me the keys, and I will finish straightening up," Lizard offered. "You go on home. You've had a bad week."

Karen stared past the doorway, absently, and said, "Yes. Thank you Lizard, I believe I will. Here are the keys. Remember, it sticks. You just have to jiggle it a bit. I'll see you Monday. Thanks again. You're a good man."

"Have a good weekend, Karen."

It was only a bit past six, but it was still winter, and Lizard noted it was nearly dark as Karen left. Lizard began putting the tom-toms, tambourines and drumsticks into their boxes, and moving them into the closet. He had been doing this for a while when he heard a voice.

"Is Miss Karen here?"

Lizard was startled, though the voice was barely louder than a whisper. He looked up to see, standing in the doorway, the small dark frame of Latisha.

"Um. No, Latisha. Karen's already gone for the evening. Can I help you with something?"

"No, sir. My grandmamma said I had to come up here and talk to Miss Karen."

"Well, maybe I will do. Will you talk to me?"

"No, sir. I don't think so."

Lizard did not speak, and the girl did not move to go.

"Latisha, would you like a fruit juice?"

"Yes, sir."

"Why don't you take off your coat and sit down."

"Yes, sir. Thank you."

Lizard got her a box of fruit punch as she struggled out of her coat, sliding onto the metal folding chair Lizard had just put back into place. He handed her the juice.

"What was it you wanted to talk to Karen about, Latisha?"

"I told my grandmamma about what I did here the other night. You know. I was.... I was upset. My grandmamma was real upset too, when I told her. And she told me I had to come down here and tell Miss Karen I was real sorry."

Lizard sat in a chair across from and identical to Latisha's, his chin in his hands as he listened. "I don't know if it helps, but I am pretty sure Karen is not mad at you. She just wants to help you be happy, but she doesn't know how."

"Mr. Lizard, I ain't never goin' to be happy, so Miss Karen don't even need to bother."

"I don't think Miss Karen would agree, Latisha."

The girl put her face in her hands, and she started to cry.

Softly, at first. And then the muffled sounds became sobs. Lizard was confused, embarrassed, helpless. Latisha cried for a full five minutes, and then she looked up, snot running down her upper lip. Lizard just looked at her.

"I'm sorry, Latisha. I am so sorry."

Latisha's face burst into fine cracks, like a breaking piece of Chinese porcelain. And a loud sob escaped her lungs.

Lizard sat without speaking, waiting patiently until the sobbing began to ebb.

"Do you feel a little better, Latisha? Sometimes crying helps, some of the hurt comes out with the tears. Did that happen for you just now."

"Yes, sir, Mr. Lizard. I do feel better. A little."

They sat in silence for several minutes, and then Latisha spoke.

"My grandmamma told me I should ask Miss Karen if she'd like to come to church with us this Sunday. She sings in the choir. I sing along from the church with the other people. Grandmamma and the choir are all up front."

"I will sure tell Miss Karen. I think she'd like to come. What church is it?"

"Emmanuel Baptist." She paused a moment. "Mr. Lizard, will you come, too?"

"I'd like that, Latisha."

"You and Miss Karen can sit with me."

THE KID AND THE POET

1

The wooden leg of the straight-backed chair groaned as the boy scooted it over the hardwood floor, a few inches closer to the bed. The room was dim, with sheer curtains allowing some gray morning light to filter in through the windows, while blocking the view of the late-autumn drizzle outdoors. The room was still, except for the coarse breaths of the old man. A stale, sweet smell hovered in the air.

Outside it was quiet. The chitter of birds littered the silence in the side and back yards. Otherwise it was quiet. Sunday mornings were always peaceful, unlike the busier weekdays, with the clatter of shops opening, children walking shrilly to school bus stops, and automobiles starting their commute to jobs on the outskirts of the small mountain town. Soon, the noise would begin to pick up a bit, as families and older couples bundled against the autumn chill would begin their walk to one of the half-dozen churches within a few blocks of downtown.

The boy had worked for the old man and his wife for a bit over a year. He had moved to the small town from another, smaller town out on the plains in the summer after his junior year in high school. That was after his parents were killed by a drunk driver. He had grown up as an only child on their small dairy farm, and he learned to work hard, helping care for the farm and the cows, and his family lived modestly but comfortably. He was a hard worker, but also thoughtful; he kept a journal in which he wrote every day.

After his parents were killed, the farm had to be sold, but for little profit. The boy was taken in by his aunt and uncle in the mountain town where they too lived quite modestly. Times were difficult for everyone after the crash of 2008.

Soon after beginning to settle into his new school, the boy started to look for a part-time job to help make ends meet. Jobs for young adults were not plentiful in the town, unless you were adept at whitewater rafting in summer or skiing in winter. The boy could milk a cow, herd cattle into a corral, or bale hay, but he could not guide a whitewater raft tour or be a ski instructor.

Every week his finger would trace down the short column of "Help Wanted" in the classified section of the semi-weekly town newspaper. For weeks there was nothing, until, "Assisted living attendant wanted. Work involves daily care for nearly bedridden patient, including personal hygiene, cooking, and general assistance. Must be able to lift and carry." That very day he called the number in the ad and spoke with a woman, who invited him to visit and interview. "Yes, ma'am. Tomorrow morning would be just fine."

The boy arrived at the house fifteen minutes before the scheduled time. It was a small bungalow, right in the middle of town, conveniently located to everything. A tidy rock garden decorated the compact front yard. A few odd, man-sized metal sculptures were placed around it. As he walked up to the door and prepared to knock, he was suddenly aware that his mouth was dry. He hesitated a moment, then rapped on the small square window in the upper portion of the door.

The woman came slowly. He could see her through the window. She was older, easily in her seventies. Her short gray hair cropped her face like the caps that his mother would wear swimming to keep her hair dry in days long gone. The woman unlatched the door and gave him a sweet smile, inviting him in for tea and to chat.

The boy took the seat at the kitchen table she offered him. The delicate china cup made a pleasant clink as she set it on the table before him. She began to pour the steaming tea from an ancient metal pot.

"My husband is dying. He has bladder cancer. It was already pretty advanced when they found it. He had surgery and radiation, but they told us there was no cure. That was about two years ago."

The boy did not know what to say. Finally, "I am sorry."

"I know. Me, too. But no way was he going to go down easily. He was determined to keep writing, and he's been writing more, at a pace like no other before.

"But now... it's just become too much. He has no energy any more. He can't fix his own boiled egg in the morning. He can't get up to sit on the living room couch to watch people passing by. He can't get himself into the tub to bathe himself, and even getting to the bathroom to relieve himself is difficult. He can't go back to his 'writing shed' in the back yard to work on his recent poems."

"I am so sorry to hear that."

"Thank you." She bit the top of her upper lip. "I tried to make up for what he can't do any more, but I can't. I can't do it anymore. I don't have the strength to help him to the bathroom, and I can't even begin to help lift him into the tub. My own back is bad. Slipped disc, and surgery three years ago. I just can't do it. That's why we decided to look for help."

"Well... I don't have any experience with helping sick people. But I am strong, and I can lift and carry someone to the bathroom, or whatever. And... I have had to learn how to boil an egg, and I can do a little more cooking than that."

"Fine," she said, grinning. "When can you start?"

"Well, I guess right away on weekends. And maybe a couple of hours in the afternoon a couple of days a week."

"Great. How about starting next Saturday. Say... 7 a.m.?"

"Wow. Sure. OK. Um... Would it be okay for me to meet your husband?"

"Of course."

2

The boy fell quickly into a routine at the old man's home. After school he went directly to the old man's house. He would sit for fifteen or twenty minutes with the old man, and he would try to chat with him, making small talk about the weather, or sports. The old man never said much. He was polite, and seemed to be listening, but rarely responding. Sometimes his silence seemed to convey only that he was annoyed.

Still, the routine developed. After their chat, the boy would help the old man with his bath. First he would fill the tub. He learned quickly the temperature the old man liked, and the woman showed him the other things he needed to learn.

Oxygen tubing trailed from his nose to a compact machine on the floor. The boy would unplug the tubing, plug it back into a small, portable oxygen tank. The tubing was long, and he carried the tank the short distance to the bathroom before returning to help the old man up and to his walker. Together they would make their way, one short, slow step at a time, inching the walker forward. When they got to the tub, the boy would remove the old man's hospital gown, put his arm around him, move the walker, and pick the old man up, gently placing him in the water. He was far lighter than the bales of hay the boy was used to tossing back on the farm.

The old man would moan at one of the few pleasures he still enjoyed. Once he was settled in the water, the boy would tenderly scrub his back and arms with a soapy wash cloth. Then his chest and legs. Last, his scrotum and, helping to rotate the old man slightly, he would gently wash his bottom.

The old woman had large, thick and very clean towels at the ready, and the boy would take one in his hands before helping the old man to his feet, and he would wrap him warmly, softly drying him. And then the journey would begin in reverse, until once again the old man was gowned and comfortably tucked into his bed. The whole adventure took nearly two hours, during which the old woman would be preparing supper. And it would be time for the boy to head home. Later in the evenings, the boy would write in his journal about his day, and about the old man.

This routine continued for several months, until the old man became too unsteady for the walk to the bathroom and the portage into the tub, and the tub baths gave way to sponge baths in the bed.

On weekends the boy spent more time at the house. There was the bathing routine, but there was also more time to chat.

One Saturday morning, during their "chat," the old man surprised the boy.

"How was school this week?"

And the boy would answer, "Good. Still getting used to a new school. It's hard. Everybody here… they all know each other already and it's not easy to make friends. I guess I am shy anyway."

"Any friends yet at all?" the old man would whisper between short, harsh breaths.

"Yeah. A couple. A couple of the guys wanted me to go out for the football team. I played for my old school, but I told them I didn't have time now."

"That's too bad. What about girls?"

"Oh, no… I don't have time."

The next few weeks were the same as before. The old man seemed even more sullen, talking less and less, and then only to answer questions. The boy just accepted this and tried not to take it personally. He assumed the man was in pain a lot of the time, until on another Saturday morning, the old man asked the boy about his plans.

"I'm sorry. What plans do you mean?"

"Well, of course I mean when you are older. Are you going to take care of dying old men the rest of your life?"

"After high school, I hope I can go on to college."

"Good. What do you want to study?"

"Well, actually I was thinking I wanted to study creative writing. I've dreamed of the program at Colorado College, if only I can get in and can afford it."

When he had first come to work for the old man and his wife, the boy had not known the old man seriously wrote poetry, much less that he was a well-known and highly regarded poet. Soon after learning this, he went off to the small library downtown and checked out three books of the old man's poetry. That night, he had stayed up until the small hours of the morning, reading those books, and he was captured, mesmerized.

At first the boy did not say anything to the old man about reading his poetry, but later, during one of their longer chats, he asked about one of the poems. "What is this really about?"

"What do you think it is about?" the old man replied.

"I am not sure."

"Then you shouldn't even be asking the question, should you?" The old man seemed angry, and the boy, feeling chastised, fell silent. This time, it was difficult not to take the old man's words personally.

3

It was early Sunday when he got to the house, but there were already three other people in the room — the old man's daughter and grandson, and of course, his wife. She had asked the boy to come and join them. Both the boy and the woman were quiet. The old man's daughter and her son were busier. Henry was only four years old, and he had no idea what was going on. Solemnity was not in his vocabulary, and his mom was responsible for keeping the decorum.

Henry's mom was a good planner. She'd brought Henry's Lego collection. And he was, mostly, involved with creating a Lego castle with Lego warriors. He sat in one corner of the room, occasionally issuing warnings that were understandable only to the Lego defenders. For the most part, though, the room was quiet.

The old man lay in the bed, his back and neck and head propped up by pillows, so that he was half sitting. He watched the others in the room with vague interest.

"May I have a sip of tea?" he whispered to his wife. These were the first words he'd uttered the entire morning.

"Yes, dear." And she rose and walked to the kitchen where there soon was the whistle of a tea kettle. She brought a steaming cup of tea to the bedside. He took the cup shakily, his wife with hands poised below, just in case, and he took a sip.

"Honey?" the old man whispered from his bed. "I think it is time now."

His wife started to weep, silently, not dramatically, just hanging her head, and letting the tears slowly run down her cheeks, and onto the sheets of the bed.

"I know," she said.

Just then, his daughter grabbed Henry's arm firmly for some Lego transgression, whispering firmly.

The old woman lifted a small plastic cup and brought a spoonful of apple sauce to her husband's lips. Then she repeated this two more times, the last after scraping clean the bottom of the cup. The old man looked at her, and said, "I love you." And to his daughter, the same thing.

And then, "Bye, Henry."

Finally, turning to the boy, he looked him in the eye, and said, "I'll see you on the other side." Then he closed his eyes. Within ten minutes, his breathing had become a soft snore, and in twenty it slowed to about four breaths a minute. Finally, there were no more breaths at all.

The boy and the two women sat in their chairs around the bed. Henry sat on the floor with his Legos, occasionally making the sounds of a revving truck. They sat in the dim light for a long time, not speaking. Even Henry was mostly quiet.

The wife was the first to move. She scooted her chair back, rose, and walked into the kitchen. The boy could hear her on the phone. "My husband has just passed away." She gave her address. When she returned, the daughter was picking up Legos, with Henry's help, and putting them in the box where they were kept.

The boy stood up and went to the wife, putting his arms around her. "I will miss him."

"So will I," she replied. "Here. He wanted you to have this." She handed him a slim book, the most recent collection of the old man's poems. The boy took the book in his hands and said thank you. "I will treasure this." Then, he slowly walked through the living room to the front door, closing it quietly behind him as he stepped onto the porch. Only then did he open the book. His name was inscribed shakily on the title page, along with the words, "Whatever you want these to mean, that is what they mean." He closed the book carefully, and stepped off the porch.

The walkway was wet, and the air smelled of fresh rain. The sun was beginning to break through the overcast. Chickadees hopped through the side yard grass, foraging for seeds. Next door, the sound of children's voices drifted from barely opened windows as they dressed for church.

HOMECOMING

He'd survived the horrors of war in southeast Asia, but it was a small town in southern Arkansas that killed him, just after he left a dark cinema on a hot August afternoon. It was 1969. The movie was *True Grit*.

He'd just turned twenty-one. He'd been home only six months. Friends who'd left at the same time as him had not returned. The few who did return — and those who never went — had all changed. They were strangers now.

It was February when he arrived home. The Greyhound from Birmingham pulled to a squeaky stop at Oscar's General Store on Main Street in Brinkley. It was late afternoon, a gray and chilly day, and drizzling when he got off the bus and retrieved his duffel bag. His mother and two sisters, standing holding to the railing, began waving when he turned back toward the store. His smile flashed his white teeth when he saw them. They were beautiful.

His momma wore her Sunday dress, and the girls were wearing their best. He stepped up onto the platform as they ran to greet him, and he engulfed his two sisters in his long, broad arms while they giggled and squealed. Then, he turned to his mother, and embraced her with a hug so tight it was as though he thought it might be their last hug forever. He got teary, and his mother was sobbing.

"I made it, Ma. I survived."

"Oh, Marvin. I ain't never been so glad to see another soul as I am you, right now. I am thankin' the Lord right now, as I breathe every breath."

Later, his body was heavy, and his eyelids. It had been a long flight and a longer bumpy bus ride after, with one transfer on the way. He felt like he could sleep for a week.

His mother had already put a pot roast in the oven. With carrots and potatoes around the sides, and a rich broth surrounding it all. He was all but overcome by the savory scent, unlike any food smell he'd had in two years, and it had been that long since she'd spent the money for pot roast as well.

In the next few weeks, Marvin began the search to find a job. He checked with Oscar at the store, hoping for maybe a clerk's position.

"Sorry, Marvin. Times are rough. I had to let one of our two clerks go just a few weeks ago."

He went to the town's Piggly Wiggly, and the manager escorted him to a room with a few desks like school desks, the ones with the table attached to the seat. Squeezed into one of the desks, he filled out a form detailing his education, background, and what kind of job he wanted. He finished the form and brought it to the girl in the small cubicle adjoining his room.

"Thank you... um (glancing at the application) Marvin. We will call you when something becomes available if you seem right for the job."

He even tried Willie Wilson at the Sinclair station. (No one knew if his name was really Willie, or just something made up to match his last name.)

"Marvin, you know I'd love to hire you. But times are so rough, I don't know how I'm gonna get by day to day. If things change, I'll sure call you."

He scanned the local paper's want ads, looking for anything he might do. The type of work did not matter much. He was used to work. Hell, he was used to a lot more than mere work. He needed a job, any job, that would give him a fair wage.

After three weeks of looking, he finally found a promising ad. Marvin's old high school was looking for a night janitor. He wrote down the phone number and called the next morning, and they set him up for an interview in two days.

It was a Thursday. He bathed in the claw foot tub the night before, and in the morning dressed in khaki trousers picked up at the thrift store for three bucks. He already had a button-down shirt and a tie. Looking in the mirror, he was satisfied.

He walked the half mile to the school. He passed by an old house with peeling paint. Evie Holcomb. She'd lived there forever. She'd been old forever. Even before he left to go to war, she was the oldest person he even knew. When Marvin walked to school, Evie would be sitting on her porch, rocking in an old wicker chair.

"Hey, Marvin," she'd call. Today was no different. She rocked in the morning sun, her frizzy gray hair sticking out everywhere.

"Hey, Marvin."

"Hey, Miss Holcomb."

Even though it wasn't terribly hot yet — it was only late March, after all — the humidity was still oppressive. He remembered when he was growing up, there was a large community swimming pool. It had a high dive, and a regular dive. He would watch with envy, walking by on his way to a friend's house, or to run an errand at the store down the street.

He watched the white kids jump joyfully the mile down from the high dive to the water below, and heard their joyful screams. Colored people weren't allowed into the public pool, and he was colored.

Later he learned that some new laws had been passed, and Marvin learned that segregation of public places was no longer legal. He was a young teen, ignorant and impressionable. The colored kids showed up that first day, and the pool was almost empty. A few kids with a few parents were there. Marvin and a dozen or so of his friends ran in the opened gate, and jumped into the pool. It was the best day of his life.

When the summer ended, the city council voted. They rejected the status of the pool as a public place. Before Halloween, the pool had been filled in, and early landscaping was started where there had once been water.

Marvin never understood. He asked his mother later why they'd closed the pool.

"It's no matter, honey. They's lots of places to swim. That hole down in Forrest Creek. That's a good swimming hole. There's no better tire swing anywhere on the river."

"Yes, ma'am."

By the time he got to the school for his interview, dark spots circled his armpits, and perspiration dripped down to his eyebrows. The school secretary rose from behind her counter in the principal's office — a familiar room. She led him down the corridor, and then the stairs to an office in a basement hallway.

Barrels neatly lined the hall, and scattered doors hid other rooms along the way. She led him to an office of sorts — a door with a frosted glass window — where she knocked.

"Come on in!" The voice was loud and authoritative. The secretary opened the door to a sparse office with a cluttered wood desk, and a single chair facing it. Marvin did not recognize the man. He was overweight, balding, in his late 40s or early 50s.

The secretary spoke. "Mr. Allen, this is the man I told you about. You should have all his papers already. He's interested in the night position. He was a student here a few years ago. A good boy."

"Well come on in. Have a seat, boy."

Mr. Allen and Marvin had a short conversation. They talked about his family, about his time in Vietnam, and about the goddamn commies everywhere.

When they had finished, Mr. Allen said, "The job is yours if you want it, boy."

"I do."

"You start next Monday, then. Come in a bit early, say... three-ish, and our day janitor, Leroy, will show you the ropes."

He rose and held out his hand while still behind the desk. "Welcome."

They shook hands, and Marvin walked out, up the stairs, and back outside, feeling relieved, if not elated. On the walk home, his step had a bit more bounce. He noticed the shade from the magnolia trees, with their glossy green leaves and their white blossoms like upturned porcelain bowls.

The next few months brought spring and, too quickly after, the hot summer bringing with it the worst drought anyone in the county could remember. Cotton wilted in the fields. The stunted cornstalks drooped. Even the soybeans looked sickly, and only the kudzu seemed to thrive.

Marvin walked to work every afternoon when he took over for Leroy, and he pushed a three-foot dry mop along all the corridors. He cleaned all the restrooms, locker rooms, and offices. The work was easier in the summer when the school was not as busy. Students still came for summer school, but many classrooms remained unused, as well as the gym and many of the administrators' offices.

It was decent money. He was glad to help his mother with expenses, and even buy her an occasional treat — flowers for the Sunday table, a small vial of floral scented toilet water. He might even have some change left for himself on some weekends if his chores at home were finished.

He also had weekends free to walk his sisters to the ball field, where they played in the softball league. He cheered for them like a father. And some days, before work, he would practice with them. He would throw pitches for them to practice hitting, or just play catch to help them learn to use a mitt. The girls laughed when he helped, and they sweated and worked hard in their practice. He shrugged at how much he enjoyed playing with them, but no father cheered louder than he when Darla hit her first home run.

He learned to cook. His momma taught him the nuances of mixing cornmeal to make cornbread with a hint of chopped jalapeño. She showed him how to slow-cook dried red beans to use for beans and rice, or almost anything. They didn't talk a lot. There was a lot he could never tell her. But he felt closer to his momma than even before the army.

It was a Saturday afternoon in August. Marvin sought shelter from the heat in the town's air-conditioned movie theater. *True Grit* would only be there one more week; afternoon tickets were cheaper. He relaxed in the chill of the theater and enjoyed the movie. When it was over, he hesitated leaving the cool, dark theater. But he had to leave, along with the fifteen or so others in the audience.

The sun was blinding when he walked out the door, but not as bad as the stifling heat. He walked to the sidewalk and turned left to head back home. It was then he heard the throaty baritone engine behind him, followed almost immediately by the squeal of spinning tires and the spitting of rocks. He turned as a beautiful GTO raged around the corner at high speed, only to slow as it approached him. A boy his age leaned out of the front, another out the back window. The driver yelled.

"Hey, nigger!"

Marvin stopped and looked toward the car. The white boy tossed an empty can out the window.

"Where do you think you're going?"

Marvin was calm. "Walkin' home, minding my own business."

"What business is that boy?"

He remembered moments like this growing up. Not many in the army though. After their first firefight in 'Nam, the skin color disappeared. Even the southern white boys learned to get along — they depended on getting along. White boys just like this one.

"I don't want no trouble. I'm just going home."

"Well maybe you better hurry on then." He revved the engine threateningly.

"I'm gonna do just that," and he turned to walk away, on down the road. The engine roared again. Once again he heard the tires and the spitting gravel. He didn't turn around, but kept walking calmly, though he could feel the muscle car coming to a stop feet away from his back. Marvin kept walking.

A few seconds later he heard the three quick pops, a sound familiar to him.

At the same instant, he felt the expansive burning in his back and chest.

And he saw the village erupt all at once, the wood and straw huts bursting in flame. Children running, screaming. Old people falling out of their burning homes, collapsing, tumbling face down onto the dirt. Some were in flames when they fell.

And then darkness descended slowly. And quietly.

BUS RIDE TO MINOT

1

The print on the ticket blurred as he stared at it in the flickering, blue-white and buzzing fluorescent light of the station's lobby. Minot. He'd never heard of Minot before his sister was stationed there over ten years ago. Even now, Adams did not even really know where it was, except that it was far north, near the Canadian border, and it was very cold.

He wandered sleepily, dragging his full duffel bag toward an empty wooden bench where he would sit until the bus began to board. Even at this late hour, the station was filled with a small crowd of people milling around, looking for seats, waiting in line for tickets, and scurrying to the restroom for a last-minute visit.

The lobby was a vaudeville of characters. A heavy black woman held a child, perhaps a bit over a year, drooling, asleep on her shoulder as she paced back and forth before the frosted window panes of the station. Two benches down from where Adams sat, a twenty-ish couple, dressed in leather and chains with high leather boots, tongue-wrestled each other furiously while pawing at each other's shoulders.

An elderly Jewish couple limped to the end of the ticket line, he with a cane in one hand, his wife's arm in the other, kippah perched atop his crown, his mid-chest beard severely silver-specked. A single large suitcase was nestled in the grip of a foldable, two-wheel carrier they pushed before them. Adams shook his head.

In addition to the duffel bag with his clothes and personal items, Adams carried a small backpack containing several books. He thought they might engage him during the long bus ride to Minot. Two novels and five or six slim volumes of poetry that had been sitting on his kitchen table, waiting to be read. But there were no medical journals, no medical texts. Adams had stopped reading those the day he retired. That was nearly two years ago.

At nearly 11:30 a voice boomed overhead. "The 11:45 bus for Little Rock will begin boarding at Gate 3 in five minutes. Five minutes." Adams began to gather his two bags, thinking of moving early to the Gate area, but already he was preceded by a horde of other waiting passengers. His hopes of getting a choice seat were dashed, not that it really mattered. It was not long before the next announcement, "The bus for Little Rock is now boarding at Gate 3; all passengers, please prepare to board now."

Adams moved to the end of the forming line. It was already long enough to suggest that the bus would be nearly full. As the line began to snake forward, Adams went through the automatic glass door and into the cold Memphis night air. His breath was immediately visible. It occurred to him, as he handed his bag to the driver for storage, that this temperature was probably balmy compared to the weather in Minot. He climbed the steps and began working his way down the aisle, past the portly bodies lifting small bags into the overhead storage. About two-thirds of the way toward the back, he angled into an empty seat, and positioned himself next to the window, settling in to continue his people-watching as others wound their way down the aisle.

Adams was not in the mood for company, and he hoped that he might get lucky, like a gambler at the roulette wheel, and have the seat beside his remain free. He was not usually in the mood for company most days lately, but especially on a long bus ride.

Surprisingly, Adams seemed to be in luck, as seats around him filled, leaving the one next to him untouched. He glanced at his watch. The bus was due to depart in two minutes. "Bingo," he thought. He would be able to stretch out, encroaching into the neighboring seat, and enjoy his solitude.

The driver climbed aboard the bus, which was already running and warm inside, and took his seat behind the wheel. The door hissed, and slammed shut, and Adams waited to hear the gears shift into reverse. Just as he was getting comfortable, the bus door hissed again, hissed open. And a young woman stumbled laughing up the stairs, exclaiming "thank you" to the driver in a voice loud enough to be heard back where Adams was sitting. She weaved her way down the aisle, scanning for a seat, and she stopped by the seat next to him.

"Is this seat taken?"

"No. You are welcome to it," he lied.

"Thank you." And she unloaded one bag on the floor in front of the seat. Stretching on her tiptoes, she lifted the other into the overhead bin. Then she took off an enormous down coat, a coat fit for an Inuit, and stuffed it on top of the bag in front of her seat. At last, she pirouetted into her seat, turned her head to Adams, and said, "Hi. I'm Penny."

2

The call had come Thursday night, two days before, at a quarter past one. Adams roused himself from a good dream, and sleepily answered the phone. It was his brother, Bruce, who lived in Ohio.

"Jack, I've got some terrible news."

"Oh, no," Adams said, waking some. "What is it?"

"It's Charlotte. No, not Charlotte, but Marie." Charlotte was their sister in Minot; Marie was her 20-year old daughter.

"What's happened?"

"Marie was in a car accident. She and her boyfriend apparently were hit head-on by a drunk driver..."

Adams felt suddenly nauseated. "So, what happened? Is she all right?"

"No... She was killed. They said she died instantly."

"Oh my god. You gotta be fucking kidding me!"

"No." Adams scarcely breathed. "I'm afraid not."

By now Adams was sitting on the side of his bed, the cordless phone pressed tight against his ear.

"No way! This can't be true."

Bruce said, "Yeah. It is true."

"Oh my god! What are we gonna do?"

"Charlotte says they are having the funeral Tuesday morning. There won't be a viewing."

"OK. OK," Adams said, trying to gather his wits. "I guess I need to make some plans pretty quick. Thanks for calling." And then, almost as an afterthought, "How is Charlotte?"

"She's pretty messed up."

"Yeah. I guess so."

Adams and Charlotte hadn't been close since they were kids. And especially after she got married in her first year in college, he felt her drift farther and farther away. Her marriage had lasted a year, maybe two — Adams couldn't remember. But she was left alone, fortunately with no kids, but with tuition and living expenses, and few solutions for financing her continued education.

Charlotte had always been the resourceful one of the three siblings. After the divorce, she began to explore ways to continue school, and she soon discovered the opportunities offered by the different branches of the Armed Forces. She explored tuition reimbursement through the Navy and the Army, finally settling on the Air Force program. Since she would graduate with a degree in nursing, she could receive a year of tuition and a living stipend in exchange for two years of service after graduation. She jumped at the opportunity, signing on for two years. Her new military lifestyle did nothing to breach the ever-growing distance between her and Adams.

After graduation and four years of practicing nursing in military base hospitals and clinics, Charlotte went back to school, again promising more time to the Air Force. And there came a second husband and then two children. Marie was the younger.

Adams' sister had become a career military person. They saw each other rarely, at a wedding or a funeral, but seldom spoke, and when they did an argument almost always ensued. She was querulous, and she was *always* right. Anyone who thought differently from her was simply wrong. It became easier just not to talk to her at all.

Charlotte and Adams had not seen each other in over ten years, and he had not seen Marie since she was four or five years old. The extent of communication between the two was a yearly electronic birthday card and a mass-mailed Christmas letter.

Adams was dreading the meeting in two days. Despite his dread, there'd only been a moment's hesitation in his decision to go. Nothing could possibly be worse than losing a child, and even his sister should not have to endure that. The bus trip was over 30 hours, with transfers in Little Rock, Kansas City, and Minneapolis. Adams would have plenty of time to prepare for the reunion.

3

Penny. He looked at her wide blue eyes and bubbly smile. How could she be in such a good mood, in a dark Greyhound bus, near midnight, on a dismally cold night in Memphis? Penny. Adams' mind began playing word games.

A penny for your thoughts.
Would you care to swap seats for a little change?
Your coat looks warm as toast, to coin a phrase.

Adams did not utter any of these, but said simply, "Hi, Penny," and reached for his backpack to retrieve a book of poetry. The bus coughed, then jerked into reverse, before moving into gear and heading toward the entrance to I-40.

"Where are you headed?" Penny asked in her singsong voice.
"Minot."
"Mine what?" she frowned.
"Minot. North Dakota."
"Oh, wow!" she exclaimed. "I never heard of it before."
"Me either. Hardly."
"So… What's in Minot?"
Adams feared he might not be reading much poetry. "Well, a huge Air Force base mainly."
"Why there?" she asked, her eyes shining interest.
"I don't know. I suppose because it is so far away from everything else. That way the Russians would probably not think to bomb it while they nuked away New York and Washington."
"Why would they do that?" she asked, a hint of anxious wonderment on her face.

Adams tested her. "Did you ever hear of the Cold War?"

"Yeah." She glanced down at her hands. "Sort of."

"Well, they flew bombers from Minot that were in the air 24 hours a day, every day. They carried nuclear bombs. And there were nuclear missiles at Minot, too. All ready to nuke Russian cities if they tried to nuke us first."

"That's pretty sick," she glanced at Adams, twisting her mouth.

"Yeah. It sure is."

After a short silence, Penny spoke again. "So, are you in the Air Force or something?"

Adams mused about his notion of teens and young adults. Weren't they supposed to be sporting iPods in their shirt pockets, with earbuds blocking out the rest of the world? He wondered where Penny's iPod was.

"No, I am not in the Air Force."

"So why are you going to Minot?"

Adams sighed. "My sister lives there."

"Oh, that's cool! So you're going to visit your sister!" Penny exclaimed with excitement.

"Yeah. Cool," Adams muttered.

The bus was easing onto the highway's entrance ramp, and soon began the crossing over the Mississippi River bridge. The lights in the bus dimmed, and a few overhead reading lights brightened down the aisle. Penny leaned forward and reached into the pocket of her oversized coat, retrieving a granola energy bar. She began to unwrap it, peeling the wrapper down to the bar's waist. She turned to Adams.

"You want half?"

"Um... No, thanks. But, thanks. Really."

"So... What's your name?"

"Adams. Jack Adams."

"May I call you Jack, Mr. Adams?"

Adams rolled his eyes. "Sure."

"So... do you have any plans with your sister and her family?"

Adams sighed again, more noticeably this time. "No, not really." He paused. And without knowing exactly why, he added, "I'm going to a funeral."

"Oh, shit. I'm sorry. Who is it?"

"My niece. She was killed in a car accident the night before last."

"Oh, God! How old is she... I mean, was she?"

"Twenty."

"Oh, shit. Same age as me."

Adams added, "Too damn young to die!"

Penny removed her knit stocking cap, freeing a tangle of frizzy, dishwater blonde hair. He could hear the crackle of static electricity as she removed the cap. She was cute, kind of. Adams wondered what her story was, but he was not about to ask.

Penny began to munch frugal bites of her granola bar, slowly and deliberately enjoying each chew. Adams could see her pleasure at the taste of each morsel of peanut, oat flake, or raisin in the half-smile of her moving cheeks and lips. This endearingly annoying young girl could be his daughter, or even grand-daughter. She was that age.

Adams again began to think of settling in, perhaps turn on his reading light and absorb a bit of poetry before dozing off.

"So ... What was your niece like?"

Adams was startled back into the moment, annoyed again. "I don't know," he replied, honestly.

Penny was silent for a few seconds, taking in Adams response. "What do you mean, Jack?"

Adams suppressed a barely audible moan. "Well... okay. If you must know, I haven't seen Marie since she was about five years old. I haven't seen my sister in over ten years."

"Damn," Penny muttered. They were silent. "Why not?"

"It's a long story."

"We have a long ride ahead of us," she replied with anticipation.

"Yeah, well... It's kind of hard to talk about."

"OK," Penny replied. Disappointment dripped like thick molasses in her voice.

Adams felt bad. He felt as though he had cut her off, when she was only trying to be interested and conversant. To redeem himself, he asked, "So, where are you going?"

"Minneapolis."

"And what's in Minneapolis for you?"

"My aunt lives there. I am going there to spend a week or so with her. My mother's sister."

"Well, that's nice. I hear Minneapolis is nice. Even though it is cold." As an afterthought, "Although I don't think it's as cold as Minot."

"I don't know. I've never been there before."

Adams was curious, but decided not to ask any more questions.

They were quiet. Eventually, he could see the city lights of Little Rock in the dark sky ahead, and soon they were pulling into the Greyhound station. The bus wheezed to a stop at one of the gates. The bus lights brightened, and sleepy-eyed passengers began moving and gathering their carry-on belongings. The bus door hissed, folding open like a Japanese fan. Adams fished out his backpack from where it was half-stuffed under the seat in front of him, and Penny stood to retrieve her bag from the overhead bin.

Just then, Adams realized that they would be boarding together the next bus to Kansas City, and then the one after to Minneapolis. He smiled slightly to himself.

4

To say that Adams' retirement was bittersweet would be half true. The truth is that his retirement was just bitter. He had practiced emergency medicine in the large ER of one of the urban medical center hospitals in Memphis for over thirty years. It had been his life, a life he loved more than he would ever have believed possible. Maybe he loved it too much. Had his long hours, and his ineptitude at leaving work at work perhaps contributed to the breakup of his twenty year marriage, now more than ten years past?

Adams had married during his residency in Cleveland, Ohio. He was happy. He thought he was happy nearly to the end, when he learned just how unhappy his wife was. Still, the knock at his door at 6 a.m. startled him, but not so much as when he saw standing on his porch the court officer with the envelop in his hand. His wife was away visiting her sister at the time, and he had no idea why a county clerk officer would be knocking at this hour. He unlocked and opened the front door of his house.

"Jack Adams?"

"Yes, sir?"

"I have papers for you. You will need to sign here."

Adams' stomach was like a pouch full of acid twisting on itself. He shakily signed the paper. And that was the beginning of the end. When Barb returned, she moved right away into a furnished apartment she had already temporarily rented, and they did not speak. Adams was left in a cavernous house that had already been too large for the two of them, and now there was only him.

Adams was not much of a fighter. "Irreconcilable differences" was fine with him. And Barb got the house, half of their joint savings, half the value of their two cars, and half of his entire pension. And Adams was so heartsick, he really didn't care. He soon moved into a small, two-bedroom apartment near downtown to try and rebuild his life. It was medicine that saved his life. After that, his vocation continued to be his source of fulfillment and his lifesaver — at least until his diagnosis.

That was just four years ago. It started with a slight tremor in his hands. Only slight, and not always present. But as it grew more frequent, he mentioned it to his internist. His physician and close friend Allen, whom he had known for years, did a basic neurological exam: finger to nose, hands outstretched with eyes open, then closed, reaching for and holding objects between fingers, handwriting sample... and more.

At the conclusion, Allen said, seriously, "I don't know, Jack. There is something there. Definitely a tremor. It's partly an intention tremor, but it seems slightly present at rest as well. It could be any of a number of things, as you know. I am going to refer you to a neurologist."

The neurologist wasted no time in arriving at a diagnosis: Stage I Parkinson's.

At first, for the first year, Adams was lucky. The tremor was not debilitating, sometimes barely noticeable, and there were no other symptoms. But with time the tremor became more pronounced, and soon Adams began having difficulties doing his work in the ER.

Procedures, in particular, were a problem. Placing central lines — large catheters into veins in the neck, groin, or beneath the collar bone — all essential to the work of an emergency medicine physician, was a challenge. At times, intubating — placing a breathing tube into a patient's windpipe — was the same sort of challenge. Adams would often have to ask the assistance of one of his colleagues.

After a time, Adams realized that he could not safely go on with his practice, and began to significantly reduce his clinical responsibilities, instead emphasizing more his teaching role. Adams knew that his disease would eventually progress, either slowly or rapidly, finally incapacitating him. And that is what led to his decision to retire early, two years ago. If he only had a few years of "quality" life remaining before the Parkinson's took over, he wanted to be sure that he enjoyed that time as much as possible.

Adams was eligible for disability, which paid 60% of his former salary. With his more humble lifestyle of apartment living, money was not an issue. There were no women to devour his paycheck, and he lived his life simply. He spent days reading and writing, reading good fiction and poetry, and writing some poetry on the side. He also cultivated a taste for fine, single malt Scotch, which he enjoyed after dinner every evening. To some it would seem a lonely life, but Adams was content. He certainly missed sex, but he was content.

5

Penny and Adams shouldered their way into the line of disembarking passengers. Adams had only his small backpack, which he loosely slung over his shoulder. Penny, on the other hand, had put on her bulky coat and stocking cap, and carried similar sized bags in each hand. As they climbed down the steps of the bus, Adams said, "Here, let me carry one of those," and

Penny gladly handed over one of the bags. Together they moved to one of the wooden benches, glancing at the bulb-lit sign silently announcing departure times for the few remaining late-night buses. It was 3 a.m. The Kansas City bus departed at 3:15.

Sitting next to Adams, Penny pulled another energy bar from her coat pocket. Again she peeled the wrapper halfway, and without speaking held it out to him. Adams felt a slight gurgle of hunger in his stomach, and said "Thanks." Penny smiled and broke the exposed half of the bar off, and handed it to Adams. He admired her foresight in thinking of food, and admonished himself for not thinking of the same for himself.

Adams rose from the bench to get a coffee from the vending machine. "Would you like a coffee?" he asked Penny.

"Sure," she smiled.

"Cream and sugar?"

"Naw. Straight up," she replied. "Black as night."

"My kind of girl," Adams smiled, and moved toward the machine. He returned with two steaming cups, hot to his fingers, and handed one to Penny.

"Thanks."

A minute passed as they blew over the hot surface of their bitter coffees, and sipped carefully. A blistered palate was not something Adams was eager to endure for the rest of the trip.

"So... Jack... What was it between you and your sister?"

He sighed once again, more reflectively this time. "I don't know, Penny. It just happened. The years passed, and we became so different that we didn't even like each other. In fact, it got so bad, we couldn't stand each other. I don't know. It doesn't make me feel good. It makes me feel sad. And a little guilty. We both dealt with it the same way. We stopped talking."

Just then, the overhead speaker: "The bus to Kansas City is now boarding at Gate 5. Gate 5 for Kansas City." Adams was partly relieved by the interruption. He and Penny gathered their bags, Adams again carrying one of Penny's. As they moved toward the glass door, Penny asked, eyes opened even wider than usual, "Jack? Is it okay if I sit next to you again?"

"Absolutely."

They retraced the steps they had taken from the Memphis bus, only in reverse, working their way toward the back, bags in tow. This bus was far less filled than the earlier one. Adams would ordinarily have been glad, for he would have been assured a seat by himself. Instead, he was glad to have Penny sitting next to him. Together they settled into a seat in almost the same location as on the previous bus.

"Would you like the window seat this time?" Adams politely asked her.

"No, thanks. I have a bit of agoraphobia. I hate feeling closed in. I need the aisle seat."

Perfect, thought Adams, as he vastly preferred the window seat and its view. It was like a re-run. He quickly tossed his backpack in front of his seat, and Penny laboriously took off her enormous coat. Again she tossed one bag in front of her seat and then began to pack the down coat in on top. Then she began the contortions in preparation for the tip-toe stretch to the upper bin for the second bag.

Adams stood up. "Here. Let me get that for you."

Penny grinned. "Thank you!" Adams returned to his seat, and Penny turned and plopped ungracefully into hers, a smile still spanning across her still fresh face. Adams watched her, and shook his head slightly with a faint smile of his own.

The bus door wheezed closed, and the gears began to grate into reverse. It was not long before they were on the highway again, headed north, and not long before Penny spoke again.

"So... you were saying?"

"I was? What was I saying?"

"About you and your sister. You both stopped talking. And you felt sad. And guilty. Why did you feel guilty?"

Adams thought a minute. "Wow. You ask tough questions, don't you?" He paused, reflecting. "I don't know. I guess you shouldn't just stop talking to your sister, you know. No matter what. Although, she stopped, too." His comment felt empty to him, as though he were trying to redirect the cause of his guilty feelings.

"No. She really did stop. But it was me who stopped *my* talking. So, it is my fault. At least half my fault."

Penny was half turned in her seat, looking directly into Adams' eyes. He felt a little uncomfortable. It was as though she were waiting for him to continue.

"I don't really have anything more to say about it."

Penny wouldn't give up. "Do you ever regret not knowing your niece?"

"If she was anything like you, then yes, I regret it."

He thought he could see Penny blush, but she was smiling. Then her face turned serious. "If I were your niece, I would really be sorry that I'd never gotten to know you."

Wow, he thought. The flattery and the guilt he felt were formidable. Adams did not say anything. He didn't know what to say.

They rode for a surprising ten minutes of silence. Penny remained half-turned in her seat, her gaze distant but not wavering. He cut his glance to the side so as to see her without being caught. She had a musing look, as if contemplating something serious and complicated. Finally, she spoke again.

"So... how will it be seeing your sister after all this time?"

Would she never stop taking him by surprise?

"I have no idea. Terrible. I will be awkward. And she will be angry, and hateful. That's how she always was. And now she has a damn good reason to be."

"Terrible? Yeah, it probably will be if you go into it thinking that way," she said.

Oh, Jesus... now she is going to lecture me? Adams didn't say anything. It was nearly 5 a.m., and soon the sky in the east, to the right, would be pinkening. This leg of the trip was a little over fifteen hours, with stops in Harrison, Arkansas, and Springfield, Missouri. But no bus transfers until Kansas City.

"Are you tired?" he asked the girl. His own eyes were starting to sting. After all, they'd practically pulled an all-nighter.

"Sort of," she replied. "Just a little."

"Maybe we should get a little shut-eye before it gets light."

"Okay. You don't seem like you want to talk anymore anyway. At least right now." She turned back in her seat, and eased the seat back into a semi-reclined position. Once again she removed her knit stocking cap, with its electric crackle. Adams watched as she settled back, closing her eyes. He wasn't so lucky. He was sleepy, but not enough to doze off at that moment. He watched his new friend, who seemed to fall immediately into dreams. He watched as her mouth gradually drooped ungracefully open, and she began quietly mouth-breathing. He watched her breathe as the eastern sky turned pink.

6

It was about 7:30 when the bus pulled into the small, single-gate station in Harrison. It pulled in and stopped without turning off the engine. After five minutes, and no departures, no new passengers, the bus ground into gear again and headed back onto the highway. Penny had not stirred. It would be an hour and a half before they arrived in Springfield, Missouri, their next stop. Adams pulled the poetry volume out of his backpack again, and began to read.

Penny continued sleeping, while Adams finished the book of poems. Springfield was a short distance off the interstate, and it was a little after nine when they pulled into the station. The driver announced that this would be a fifteen minute stop, and if anyone wanted to exit and stretch their legs, it would be fine.

Adams' stomach was audibly growling now, and he decided to see what could be bought for breakfast inside the terminal. He managed to step over Penny's coat and bag, taking care not to jostle her knees as he crawled past her. He tried hard not to waken her, and was pleased that she did not budge; her eyelids did not even flutter.

Inside, Adams was surprised. Just past the rotating door was a short order grill. Possibilities were more numerous than he'd dared hope for. Pancakes, bacon and eggs, bagels and cream cheese. Adams asked the cook if he could make an egg, cheese and sausage sandwich on an English muffin. The cook replied, "Oh, yeah. Just like an Egg McMuffin. Of course I can."

"I'll take two," Adams said, "and two large coffees. Black."

"Yes, sir. Five minutes." Adams wandered to the end of the line, and picked up a copy of the morning's *Springfield News*.

When the sandwiches were ready, he took the bag to the register at the end of the counter, paid, and returned to the bus. Penny was awake. "Good morning, sunshine," he greeted.

"Hi." She took the sandwich from the bag he handed her. "Oh, thank you!" She beamed at him.

"You missed the sunrise," Adams told her. "It was actually quite pretty. The flat land gave us a plain view of the sun coming up from behind the horizon — no pun intended."

Penny giggled as she unwrapped her sandwich. "I was having some crazy dreams," she said between mouthfuls.

"Oh, really? What were they?"

The motor of the bus turned over, and the last stragglers of passengers re-boarded the bus, along with a few newcomers.

"I don't really remember exactly, at least not a lot of details. There was a big bird, a big beautiful bird, like a swan, only bigger. And it had multi-colored feathers, like a peacock. It was really beautiful, and it was floating down this pretty, calm stream, with clear water that reflected the sunlight.

"As it moved down the stream, I could see a huge whirlpool, or something, right in its path. It was like in a bathtub while it drains, only bigger. The bird was floating right toward it, but didn't even notice. And then suddenly the bird was caught in the outskirts of the whirlpool, and it got whipped around, fast, in a circle. It looked back at me, and there was terror in its face. I wanted to help, but there was nothing I could do. And around and around, the water whipped the bird around in smaller and smaller and faster circles until all at once, at the very center, the bird got sucked under."

"Wow. That's pretty powerful. What do you make of it?"

"It made me feel very sad, very sad that this beautiful bird died so terribly, looking at me for help. Only I couldn't. And I felt guilty. I wanted to cry. In fact, I think I may have cried in my sleep."

"That's pretty heavy. You should probably think about that one some more."

"Yeah." Her smile faded into a distant look. She took another bite of her sandwich, and a sip of her coffee, looking blankly ahead. Adams was quiet. He did not say anything, wouldn't have known what to say if he had wanted to. He also took another bite of his sandwich, pleased that it actually tasted better than an Egg McMuffin.

They rode in silence for ten more minutes, until their sandwiches were finished, and their coffees nearly so. Adams was surprised that he found himself wanting conversation, more conversation. So he took the risk and struck it up.

"Don't you have an iPod? I thought everyone your age had an iPod, and that their ears are never separated from their earbuds."

"I have an iPod, but I left it at home." As an afterthought, she added, "On purpose."

"Oh, yeah? Why's that?"

"Somehow it didn't seem like this was the right kind of trip for iPod music."

"Why's that?"

Penny shrugged, "I don't know. It just didn't."

Adams felt he was treading on sensitive ground, and changed the subject to one more comfortable to him. "Do you like poetry?"

She said, "Oh, yeah. I am not too fond of some of the old fashioned rhymey stuff like they mostly teach you in school. But I like some of the modern poets that I have read."

"Oh, really?" Adams perked up. "Who have you read? What do you like?"

"I have read e.e. cummings. I like some of his stuff. Kind of weird, but pretty fun. And someone told me I should read William Carlos Williams, that he was the father of modern poetry. I liked everything of his I read, like 'The Red Wheelbarrow.' Pretty amazing — so much said with so few words. Someone else told me to read Sylvia Plath. I did, and she blew me away, but some of her poems were too scary and too depressing."

It was Adams who was blown away. He would never have guessed that this 20-year old girl would know these poets. He was impressed. "Would you like to read some of what I brought with me?"

"Oh, yes! I really would!" Her exuberant smile had magically reappeared. Adams retrieved from his backpack the book he had just finished. It was a volume of poems by his favorite poet. He handed it to Penny, and said, "Try this. He may be a little different from what you've read before, but I think you will like him. He is not overly complicated, and his images are like magic. He was the poet laureate for the United States for two consecutive terms back in the mid-90's. If he is not to your liking, that's OK; I won't be offended."

She eagerly took the paperback from him. "Thanks." Adams reached back into his backpack and took out another thin paperback — a short novel recommended by several of Adams' friends. He had chosen that as one of his novels for this trip. Kansas City was about three hours' reading time away, with a few short stops along the route, but no transfers. Adams and Penny both settled into their reading.

The ride was pretty boring, without the conversation, but the reading was good. Adams was hooked by his novel with the first page. Penny seemed equally engrossed, slowly and deliberately reading each poem, and then rereading. A couple of times, during moments when Adams rested his eyes and adjusted his reading glasses, he noticed her turning the pages back to an earlier poem, already read. He was pleased.

Adams had purchased two bottles of water in Springfield, and he reached into his backpack and fished them both out. He opened one, and handed it to Penny. And then he opened the other for himself. Penny took the bottle without lifting her eyes from the page.

The traffic was starting to get heavier. They were getting close to Kansas City. They would have to transfer to another bus there, and maybe have time to grab a bite of lunch.

Penny gently closed the book of poems, and let out a long, slow sigh. Adams wasn't sure what the sigh meant. He turned to her and asked, "So?"

"He is unbelievable! He creates images with words that are absolutely alive, perfect, with such detail. Images of things that are common, everyday things. But in his hands, it is like magic.

They become something much more than words, so much more than everyday things. They become sad so I want to cry. Or funny, so I want to laugh out loud. Or just mystifying. They leave me feeling like I just left a wonderful church service. Like God just winked at me, or something."

Adams felt something inside his chest. She had just described how the poems made him feel as well, and he was thrilled that she had enjoyed them so much. He also felt, oddly, proud of her.

He was jarred back to the noonday winter sun of Kansas City by the hiss of the bus pulling into the station, a station far bigger than any of the previous ones. Once again, they gathered their belongings and headed up the aisle. Inside, the terminal was crowded and dingy, but right next door and adjoining, there was a small food mart, like the ones in malls, and an open area with tables. A Burger King and a Subway were the first to grab their attention. Adams looked at Penny and asked, "Care for a Subway, *mademoiselle?*"

"*Mais oui, merci.*"

So… she could speak French too, even if only a little?

7

After Adams and Penny finished their Subways and Cokes, it was time to find their next bus. Adams scanned the notification screen, and found the bus bound for Minneapolis. They walked to the gate, and the waiting passengers were more numerous than at the last station. Together, Adams and Penny took a seat on a bench near the door, and when the boarding announcement came, they quickly took a position near the front of the line. Neither wanted to take a chance on not sitting together.

The sliding glass door opened, an attendant checked their tickets, and another took their checked bags to load into the belly of the bus. Adams and Penny took their carry-on bags and worked their way toward the back of the bus, and claimed squatters' rights in nearly the same spot as in the previous two buses. And then the same ritual of placing bags into the overhead bin and on the floor, and they took their seats. Soon the new bus was on the road again. This leg was a little over eight hours, with one stop in Des Moines. It would be long after dark before they arrived in Minneapolis.

Adams started the conversation this time. "Penny, what are you going to do in Minneapolis?" He realized that he knew next to nothing about her, nor her immediate plans, though he did realize that her massive coat prepared her well for the cold of Minnesota's February.

"I don't know," she replied, speaking into her hand as much as to Adams. "I guess I'll be doing whatever Aunt Elizabeth has planned pretty much."

"How well do you know your Aunt Elizabeth?" Adams ventured.

"Not all that well. She was kind of the black sheep in my mom's family. She never married. She works with investments, or something. Never married, but lots of boyfriends over the years, from what I hear. She is free-spirited.

"I only see her every couple of years when the family gets together for the holidays or something, not very often at all. She seems pretty cool."

"Sounds like you might enjoy your time with her," Adams offered.

"Yeah." Penny did not sound too convincing, but Adams let it go.

Penny was silent for a long while. Adams left her to her thoughts, and plucked the second novel from his backpack, since he'd finished his first before they arrived in Kansas City. Penny's energy was changed. She was immersed in thought. Even though Adams didn't really know her, he sensed something was different.

"A penny for your thoughts," he tried, half smiling.

Penny half-smiled in return; she caught the pun, but she said only, "Nothing. I'm not really thinking anything." Penny may have fallen for the pun, but Adams did not fall for her reply. He wondered what she was thinking, why her exuberance had become so serious. But once again, he let it go.

"Would you like to try this?" He offered the first, shorter novel to her. Penny said, "Sure," and accepted the paperback from him. And they both sank into their respective books. They rode reading in silence for an hour, and then Penny struggled from her seat, saying she needed to pee, and she began working her way down the aisle to the back of the bus.

Adams had a fleeting thought about his own hygiene at the moment. He was used to a daily morning shower, more to help wake up than for personal cleanliness. But somehow eighteen hours riding a bus, passing in and out of dirty bus terminals, made him feel grimy. He wished the bus had a shower.

Penny returned and climbed in over the coat and bag in front of her seat. The window next to Adams' cheek was cold, like ice, and its bottom was made translucent by a narrow band of frost. The landscape beyond the window was nearly flat, with the remnants of summer cornfields, stalks now leafless; furrows between the rows were dark earth pocked with patches of snow. The sky was bullet gray.

They rode another hour, reading in silence. And Adams asked, "Penny, are you okay?"

"Yeah, I'm okay. I'm just reading." Adams was not convinced.

Adams returned to his book, but the 24 previous sleepless hours caught up to him, and he began to drift, soon fully dozing despite his efforts to keep reading. He continued to doze fitfully, losing his place in the book, for an hour.

"Jack? Jack, are you awake?"

Adams found himself back on the bus sitting next to Penny, and he smiled. "I am now," he answered.

"Jack..." She stared at her open hands in her lap. "Jack, I am pregnant."

Adams sat upright, suddenly fully awake, and his book slipped to the floor in front of his seat. "What? Um, really? I mean, um... Congratulations. Right?"

Penny was half-turned in her seat again, looking straight into his eyes. Adams was suddenly speechless, though he felt a pressure to say something more. Penny spoke first. "No. No congratulations. It's not good."

"Oh," he said, sounding dense. "Do you want to talk about it?"

"I don't know," she hesitated. "I feel so stupid."

Adams waited. Penny continued, "I feel so stupid. I have had only one serious boyfriend. We were together, dating, for two years..."

Adams waited.

"I thought we would be together forever. Probably get married, you know? We just couldn't, not right now. And when we started, you know, having sex... making love... we were very careful to time it around my periods, so this wouldn't happen. He didn't like condoms. I guess our timing wasn't all that great, was it."

Adams felt as out of place as a circus clown at a Catholic mass. He wasn't sure what to say at all. So he remained quiet.

"When he found out I was pregnant, he was really upset. Angry. He said he didn't want it. The baby. I was very confused, and I told him I didn't know what to do. He told me I should figure it out, and then I didn't hear from him for three days. When he finally called, he was still angry, and he asked me what I'd decided. I didn't know what he meant, and I didn't know what to say. I hadn't even told my mom yet. He told me to figure it out. That was the last time I heard from him, over a week ago."

Now it was Adams turn to twist in his seat. He looked Penny directly in the eyes, and asked, "Did you tell your mom?"

"Yeah. She was really pissed. She said that I had to get an abortion, but she didn't want me to do it in Memphis. So she was the one to arrange my trip to see Aunt Elizabeth. My aunt knows lots of people, and one of her friends works at this clinic. That's why I am going to Minneapolis."

Adams kept looking her in the eyes. He felt completely out of his element. He was used to difficult conversations from his years in the emergency room. He had mastered the art of being both factual and compassionate, and he'd learned the art of listening. But this was different. Here was this young woman he'd known not even 24 hours, and she was telling him a story he'd never dreamed hearing — her story.

Following his instincts, he asked her, "How do you feel about all of this?"

"I am really pissed at my so-called boyfriend, for starters. At my mom, too. She never really talked to me about it. She really didn't give me any choice, not that I would have chosen different."

Adams pressed a bit more, gently. "How do you feel about the abortion?"

Penny replied quickly, "Scared."

Adams waited, then asked, "Scared of what?"

Penny wavered. "Scared of… Will it hurt?"

And then, quickly, "No. That's not what scares me. I am scared of how I am going to feel afterward."

Adams continued gazing into her royal blue, serious eyes. "What do you mean, Penny?"

"I don't know," she continued. "I mean… How will I feel when it's gone, and it was my decision?"

For a fleeting moment, Adams wished he'd trained in psychiatry instead of emergency medicine. But he did at least know that asking open questions was usually a good thing, a helpful thing.

"How do you think you will feel, Penny?"

"I'm not sure." And they fell again into silence. Adams was not sleepy any more. He was alert, and thinking deeply.

They rode in silence for what seemed like a long while, both apparently in deep thought. From the little Penny had shared with him, Adams wasn't sure if this was all her choice. He wasn't even sure if she knew well enough what her choice would be, if it were hers to make. It sounded more like this was a choice her mother and her boyfriend had made for her. And he felt bad for her to be in such a lonely position, at the beck and call of others. He wanted to be helpful, but he didn't know how.

"Penny, I just don't know what to say. I have so many thoughts spinning around in my head, but no words for them. I feel so bad for you, and I'd like to be helpful. How can I help?"

"You can't help, Jack. No one can. I am in this all alone."

Adams turned back in his seat, facing forward again. He glanced out at the still barely rolling farm fields and the gray sky. It was nearly 4:30, and it was already starting to get dark. He caught sight of a lighted sign announcing 20 miles to Des Moines. He was suddenly aware that he was hungry again, and he wondered what he might be able to find to eat in the station in Des Moines. It would only be a 15-minute stop, so he wouldn't have long to decide, as if there would be much to decide upon any way.

Without looking, Adams could feel Penny staring straight ahead at the back of the seat in front of her. "Penny," he looked at her, "are you OK?"

"Yeah…" Then, "No."

"I am sorry. I'm sorry for you."

"Don't be. It's my fault. I was so stupid."

They fell back into silence for the rest of the way into Des Moines. When they arrived, Adams said, "Hey, I am going to see what they have to eat. Want to join me and stretch your legs?"

"No. I think I'll stay here."

Disappointed, and concerned, Adams stepped over Penny and her luggage, and made his way inside the terminal. It looked a bit like the station in Kansas City, and a bit like the one in Springfield. There were not many people, but there was a grill. Adams ordered two hamburgers, two fries, and fixed two cups of Coke from the fountain. After paying, he returned to the bus and wound his way back to his seat, handing Penny her bag and cup, while again climbing over her to his seat. Before they spoke, the bus was in reverse, and then headed back to the highway. In another four hours they would be in Minneapolis.

Adams and Penny both chewed their burgers and fries in silence. Adams was sipping on the straw of his Coke when he heard Penny. "Thanks."

"You're welcome," he answered.

When they'd finished, they both wiped their fingers on their napkins and stuffed them along with the wrappers into one of the two sacks, and that sack into the second, which Adams pushed between his seat and the wall of the bus.

The bus was soon dark, with the "ambient lighting" only, and a few overhead reading lights dotting the ceiling along the two rows of seats. Adams leaned a bit toward Penny's seat. "Penny, may I ask you a question?"

"Sure. I guess."

"I was wondering how you feel about this abortion. I mean, is this something you want? Or is it something your mom wants?"

She was thoughtful for a moment, and then she answered, "Well, my mom wants it for sure." A pause, and then, "I am not sure what I want."

"Penny, I am no expert. I am not even a father, no kids, and if I did have kids they would probably be boys, so I still wouldn't be much of an expert. But there is one thing I know, I think I know, that is true in many kinds of situations."

"What's that, Jack?" Penny asked, now really interested.

"I think it is really important that every person faced with a difficult choice follow the path that they feel right. Not the path that somebody else feels is right, but that they, themselves, truly believe is the right choice.

"If you feel that the abortion is the right thing for you, then don't doubt yourself. If you think it is not the right thing for you, then don't let someone else make your decision for you.

"Either way, you have the strength within you to figure out what is right. And then you have the strength to make the choice work for you, even if it is a challenge."

She didn't say anything further.

8

The bus arrived at the terminal in downtown Minneapolis a little past nine. The lights of the bus came on, and people began foraging for their belongings. Adams and Penny repeated their now familiar ritual. Penny put on her coat, and this time her cap as well, retrieving it from the large pocket. Adams helped her with the bag in the overhead bin, and they joined the others working their way to the front, Adams carrying his backpack and one of Penny's bags.

When they got inside, they wandered over to where their checked bags would be brought. Penny looked around, searching, a bit anxiously. In a few minutes the passengers' bags were brought in on a large cart. Adams retrieved his duffel bag, and Penny her suitcase, and they stepped back from the rest of the small crowd. Penny looked around, then suddenly started waving. Near the exit of the terminal, also waving, was a middle-aged woman who looked nothing like Penny.

Only then did Penny turn back to Adams. She threw her arms around him and hugged him more tightly than he ever remembered being hugged. When they finally separated, he saw tear tracks on Penny's cheeks. She said, "Bye, Jack," and turned abruptly and walked toward where her aunt was standing.

Jack stood alone, and watched as her figure already seemed to grow smaller and distant. Halfway to her aunt, Penny suddenly turned and yelled loud enough for everyone to hear, "Jack! Jack! Good luck with your sister!"

9

Adams found the gate for the bus to Minot, which was leaving in 45 minutes. It was now habit: when the time came, he showed his ticket to the attendant, he dropped his duffel bag on a pile of luggage waiting to be loaded, and climbed the steps of the bus. Hardly anyone was aboard, and the line behind him had been short. Four uniformed youngsters and a few other stragglers. The bus would be almost empty. And, also by habit, Adams moved to the seat that would have been his and Penny's.

Adams tossed his bag and coat on the aisle seat, and sat down, half sideways, in his window spot, sprawling into the adjacent seat. He pulled out his book as the bus started and began backing out of the gate. His overhead reading light on, he picked up where he'd left off — *The Road*. Cormack McCarthy.

It was very different traveling alone. Adams had always thought that this was his preference, choosing whenever possible the seat with an empty one beside. And if this seat were occupied, he would choose not to speak, or to speak as little as possible. Now, he missed Penny beside him, and even though absorbed in his novel, he couldn't help being distracted by thoughts of this vivacious, joyful, and very sad young woman. He wondered how she would be. He thought that she would be okay.

For the next eight hours, Adams dozed and read. Once he got up to go to the bathroom in the back of the bus and pee. Twice he opened a bottle of water to sip while he read. Time passed slowly, and he was wistful.

Around 5:30, the eastern sky behind the bus began to brighten. It was still cloud-covered, and it looked cold. In another half-hour, they were pulling into the small Greyhound Station in Minot. Adams waited until the other passengers had finished gathering their belongings and had exited the bus. His intestines felt like someone had tied them in a knot, and his mouth was drier than he ever remembered.

He put on his jacket, slung the backpack over his shoulder, took a deep breath, and headed to the door. He was not even sure what his sister looked like.

COMING HOME

Today was the day he'd dreaded. Also, the day he'd ached for.

Thanks to the remote starter, the car would be warm. There was nothing to gather but some warm sweaters and an extra coat, just in case. He glanced at his wife, nodded, and they headed to the door.

The cold air shocked his face as they stepped out the door and down to the steps to the car. He could see his white breath before his graying beard, which was beginning already to feel brittle from the cold. Sheppard-Pratt Hospital was a 45-minute drive from the county, and the thought of the silence during the drive unnerved him. But so did the thought of conversation.

Elizabeth was prepared. Properly dressed, perfectly in control. She'd packed a hand-carried cooler with sandwiches. You can always offer food to sick people. It may make them feel better, or not. It does make the giver feel better.

Erica had been in the hospital for over two months. It had been longer than that since he and Liz had talked much. They'd been cordial, and carefully non-confrontational. He wondered if they'd been afraid of what might erupt from a real conversation.

He carried the cooler down the stairs to the car, and Liz followed, sweaters and jacket in hand. Moving to the right of the car, he opened the door for his wife. Glenn was not inclined to be so thoughtful, but today seemed different. Liz tossed the clothing into the back beside the cooler. They buckled their seat belts and he headed the car toward the highway, toward the hospital. The hum of the tires on asphalt was calming.

"Glenn?" She looked over at the driver. "What if she's not ready?"

"What do you mean?"

"I mean... what if she's not ready to be out." Her gloved hands fidgeted in her lap. "You know? On her own? How do we know something won't happen again?"

He stared at the road ahead. "I don't know."

The road noise became more rhythmic and pronounced as they sped up the ramp and onto the highway.

"What if she comes home, and something happens again?"

"I don't know, Liz. That's what the doctors are supposed to figure out. If she were not okay to come home, they wouldn't let her, would they?"

"No. I guess not."

His mind was racing as they sped up the ramp onto Interstate-175. How could he be sure? How did he really know if the doctors had figured it out? Was she ready to come home? His grip on the wheel tightened, and he merged aggressively into the next lane as they joined the highway traffic.

"The doctors do the best they can, and they wouldn't let her go before she was ready, right?" she asked, pleading.

"Yes. You're right. We'll be okay." He sighed, and his fingers drummed on the steering wheel.

The half-hour drive to the hospital was familiar, but today it seemed to take longer. Their conversation slipped into silence after they'd blended into the traffic. Liz was not in the mood to talk. Neither was he.

The highway raced beneath the car making soft, thumping sounds, like sounds from a dryer drying tennis shoes. The road needed repaving. He drove with determination — not speeding, but resolved to let no one interfere with the drive. The space between them made him think of pictures of the Grand Canyon — a great expanse, with an abyss below. His eyes burned.

"Do you want a coffee before we get there?"

She said nothing. He glanced over, settling back in his seat. She was holding her iPhone, looking at him before snapping a silent photo of him driving. Annoyed, he looked back to the highway ahead, wet from the salty mush left over from last week's snow.

He gazed toward the road and the traffic, but his mind saw the backyard pool that summer day eight months ago. They were barbecuing, enjoying the cool pool water, Robbie in his "water wings." They were all laughing — his wife, Liz, Erica and Robert Sr.

Glenn was tending burgers on the grill. Robert had joined him. Beers in hand, they chatted emotionally about the Orioles' pitching staff, and the weakness of their bullpen. Erica and Liz lazed by the pool, talking, sipping samosas.

In the snap of an instant from hell, Erica's scream pierced the backyard.

"Where's Robbie?"

Pandemonium. They flew from lawn chairs, sending them flying. Glenn nearly knocked over the grill. Within seconds they all spied the dark shape at the bottom of the pool. The boy hovered motionless, and both Glenn and Robert dove in. They grabbed him, pulling him to the surface, and then to the side of the pool. The boy was motionless, and his face and lips were blue.

Glenn knew CPR and immediately started giving the boy breaths, bellowing for someone else to call 911. He remembered how the boy's chest filled and rose, more easily than he'd expected. And after several breaths, he began pressing on the boy's chest.

"Robert. Do the chest compressions!" And the boy's father took over with surprising competence, while Glenn continued to fill the boy's lungs with air.

In minutes that seemed like hours, the medics were there, taking control, and they took over compressing Robbie's chest. Then they opened his mouth to insert a breathing tube and hooked the tube to an oxygen bag, using it to inflate the boy's lifeless lungs.

They lifted the boy and placed him on a gurney, still performing CPR, rolling him to the back of the ambulance. With a blaze of blue and red, and the fury of the siren's wail trailing behind, they were gone.

Glenn started, as if from a dream. Liz was pointing to the signs for I-695. "Glenn?" He rounded the exit and merged onto the new interstate. Within minutes they were at the gates of the venerable hospital, where after polite questioning at a guard post, the attendant waved them on past the green and grassy grounds to the parking lot before the hospital.

Glenn turned the car off and looked toward his wife. "Are you ready?"

"Of course."

Together they began the walk up the steps to the formidable wooden door, much like a wooden door barricading an ancient castle. A well-dressed receptionist met them and escorted them into a waiting area. The room was adorned with expensive-looking, oversized couches and easy chairs. The ornate ceiling appeared thirty feet tall, and the plush velour drapes trimming the enormous windows cascaded from ceiling to floor.

After what seemed forever, two nurse's aides appeared with a woman who was barely recognizable. Her face was pale, and gaunt. Her hair was combed straight back, but not into her familiar ponytail. She wore a simple navy-blue skirt and plain white blouse, and ambled toward them, shuffling.

"Mom?" The woman whispered, looking vacantly at Liz. Then she approached her, and hugged her mother tentatively. Liz embraced her back, and hugged her like a bear.

After a full minute, the woman looked aside at her father.

"Dad?" She moved toward him and parted her arms to give him a hug. As she lifted her arms to do so, he saw the redness of her left forearm, and the scars of recent stitches extending from her wrist half way up to her elbow, like steps on a ladder. Glenn stomach turned, and he felt a hint of tears sting his eyes. He hugged her tight, even as he felt her stiff body holding back.

Erica drew her head back. "Dad, you make me think of him. Of Robbie." Her eyes filled with unfalling tears, and Glenn looked into them silently.

"Erica, I'm sorry."

Liz stood in the distance. She brushed her hair back with her hand.

"He was my son."

"I know, Erica. He was my grandson."

One of the aides stepped forward, pushing a cart holding a large suitcase.

"Excuse me," she whispered, interrupting. "Here is your luggage."

Glenn reached behind his daughter and lifted the suitcase from the cart.

"Are you ready?"

"Yes, Daddy." Erica put on her coat, and they moved toward the mammoth door. Crossing the parking lot, no one spoke. When they got to the car, Glenn lifted the heavy suitcase into the trunk, then opened the front door.

"You sit in front, Erica," his wife spoke up. And their daughter climbed into the front passenger seat, while Liz opened the back door.

Outside the car, all looked grey. Glenn got into the driver's seat, gripped the wheel, and looked out on the lot. Dirty darkstained snow banks. Some white snow, black asphalt. Everything looked grey.

"Everybody ready?" He glanced around at his passengers. Erica stared out the side window. Liz replied, "Yes. Let's go."

He started the engine and pulled out of the lot and onto the driveway, heading toward the guardhouse guarding...something; he wasn't sure what. Within minutes, they were back on the highway, headed toward home, the silence deafening.

Erica continued staring out onto the grey scene passing by. He turned on the radio, to the local NPR station. Barber's "Adagio for Strings," and he melted into the seat. He shook his head as he heard the sad strains of violins. No one said a word.

When they got to the house, Glenn carried the bag to the upstairs guest room. It was the same floor as his and Liz's bedroom. The proximity seemed a good idea. It would be easier for them to notice if something was not right.

He walked into their bedroom. Framed photos, not there a year ago, adorned the bureau and the two nightstands. Robbie, tearing wrapping paper from a Christmas gift. Robbie, asleep, curled against their Golden Retriever. Robbie, in his high chair, birthday cake smeared on his face, Erica and Robert on either side.

He sat, somber, on the side of his bed, one of the photos in his hands. His grandson. Robbie was his grandson.

Downstairs, Erica shuffled into the kitchen from the back porch without a word. She moved a bar stool closer to the breakfast counter and sat down. Her gaze was forward and empty when her father came back from upstairs.

"Mom, have you heard anything at all from Robert?" She glanced at her mother. "Tell me the truth."

"Oh, honey." She moved toward her daughter and embraced her from the side. "The last time we heard from him was right after he got to Fairbanks. We told you. He called when he heard about ... when he heard you were in the hospital. I don't know how he heard. He said he would be in touch."

"Has he? Has he been in touch?"

"No, honey. Not since then. We haven't tried to call him either, mainly because we don't know his number."

"But that was almost four months ago!" Her bottom lip quivered.

Liz didn't speak and looked lost. "But you two were about to kill each other. Right?"

Erica buried her face into her hands and sobbed.

Liz and Glenn did not know details. But they could see that things were not good after the accident. Erica and Robert didn't talk to each other, or anyone. Or, when they did talk to each other, they were angry, hateful. Robert started drinking. Every night. Erica, too, not long after. And then, with no warning, Robert announced that he was going to visit his brother, who lived in Fairbanks. In less than a week, he had packed and he left. Erica was alone in that house.

Glenn came into the room from upstairs and turned to the sink, turning on the faucet and filling a glass with water. He heard the last of the conversation between the two girls.

Erica wiped her eyes and nose, raised her head.

"I was so angry. And so was he... But I wasn't angry at him."

"I didn't know it, but I was angry at me. And at you, and Robert, yes. And even at Robbie, and... more. I don't know who..."

She took a deep breath, and no one spoke. For nearly fifteen minutes, no one said anything. Glenn put dishes away in the cabinet. Liz and Erica sat staring across the breakfast counter.

"I thought I'd make 'quick-chili' for dinner. Is that okay?" Quick-chili was code for a special, family comfort food they'd concocted over the years. Canned beans, canned tomato sauce, hamburger, and so forth. It could be assembled and cooked in less than an hour.

"That would be great, Glenn." Liz spoke first.

Erica mumbled. "Just like old times. I like it." She then added, "I need to go upstairs, clean up and change."

Liz chirped. "Yes! Of course. The main bathroom is all clean. Your dad and I have the one in the master bedroom, so the one in the hallway is all yours." They'd been careful to prepare the bathroom, removing all razors and blades, and any medications or cleaners that might be a problem. They even threw out a can of Comet cleanser.

"There are towels in the cupboard next to the toilet."

Glenn fidgeted. "Okay. I'll get to work on dinner."

Erica got up and walked toward the stairs.

"Let us know if you need anything, honey." Liz's voice lilted like a child's song.

Glenn and his wife stood silent for minutes, staring at each other, until they heard the upstairs bathroom door close.

"What do you think?"

"How do you think she is?"

They spoke both at the same time, and Glenn smiled.

"I don't know," he ventured, his smile vanishing.

"Me either."

She reached across the counter and touched his forearm. "I'm scared."

Glenn's lips were pursed. Together they fumbled with dinner preparations, and they were both relieved when they heard the bathroom door open and close a half-hour later.

That night, after dinner and clean-up, the three — mother, father, and daughter — took seats in the large living room. Glenn turned on CNN as the women found blankets or Afghans and claimed their space on one of the two couches. The big-screen TV cast its blue, hypnotic spell on the room.

Glenn trusted CNN as much or more than any other news

broadcast, except perhaps NPR. But for "constant" news, Glenn turned to CNN. His choice was no surprise to Liz. Erica had curled into one side of one of the couches, bundled in a blanket. Her mother, like a mirror image, curled into the other side, wrapped in her own blanket. They both were quiet as they watched the news, the anchor and four panelists arguing about politics.

As one show transitioned into the next, Glenn glanced at the two women, and then at his watch. Both women were asleep, Liz with her mouth open. It was only ten.

"Liz? Erica? It looks like we're all three tired. Why don't we head upstairs?" Both women stirred, and they opened their eyes sleepily. Erica stretched.

"Sounds like a good idea."

They folded their blankets, and Glenn pointed the remote to turn the TV off before the three shuffled up the stairs.

"Good night, Erica." Liz glanced back as her daughter was closing her bedroom door. Erica did not reply.

Glenn was already brushing his teeth at one of the two sinks when Liz came in and began to wash her face at the other. Neither one spoke.

Glenn crawled into the bed and pulled the blankets up to his chin, lying on his side at the left of the bed. Liz joined him some minutes later, and he saw the lights turned out. They lay, back to back, not speaking. Soon, he recognized the regularity of her soft breathing, while his eyes remained open, staring into the dim blackness of the bedroom. He could hear the slow tick of the grandfather clock in the hallway.

He could not be sure how much time passed. It seemed like an hour. Perhaps more. He lay awake, on his side. Finally, he moved his legs to the side of the bed, and to the floor. And he fumbled on the nightstand until he found the photo he knew was Robbie, eating his birthday cake with his parents. He took the picture, left the bed, and found his bathrobe. His watch showed 1:15.

He shuffled quietly to the door and the dim nightlight in the hallway, and then made his way downstairs. In the kitchen, he turned on the light, and poured himself a glass of milk, then took a seat at the breakfast counter. He set the photo on the counter before him, and he looked at it.

Robbie was his grandson, too.

GROUP

Her dyed blonde hair was pulled back, leaving her with a stern hairline on her forehead. Somewhere in her mid-forties, probably.

"Hello, everyone. First, a welcome to our new guests. We are sorry for you having to be here, but glad you have taken this important first step." Her words sounded rehearsed.

"Just a reminder of a few rules... First, anyone here may speak. But if you don't feel like talking, you don't need to. If you do speak, however, please be considerate of others who might also wish to, and leave time for them.

"Next, remember that anything mentioned in this room is private and must not be shared. You may share with each other outside of our meetings, but not with others who are not in our group.

"Last, it is normal to have strong emotions as we talk. If you wish to cry, then cry. We have plenty of tissues." She smiled. "If you feel angry, that is normal, and it is okay to express it.

"If you feel you need to step out for a minute, that is also okay. Either I or Bob, my co-facilitator may come check to be sure you are all right." She waved her arm toward a younger man sitting opposite her in the circle of chairs. He nodded in bashful greeting.

"For our new group members, we begin our meetings by lighting a candle, introducing ourselves, and saying a few words about our children. Carol, would you like to start?" She looked toward a dark-haired woman sitting to her right.

There were ten people in the room, including the two who appeared to be the facilitators. Among the other eight were six women and two men. Erica looked keenly at each one, trying to read their eyes. One man appeared to be a partner with the woman sitting next to him. She couldn't be sure about the other.

"My name is Barbara. I light this candle in memory of my baby girl, Sophie. She turned four just two weeks before..." She paused and took a breath. "Before she ran out into the street." She flicked the switch on the plastic "candle," obviously a Dollar Store purchase. She set it on the coffee table in the center of the circle before sitting back in her chair, her eyes glassy and staring straight ahead.

To her right sat an older woman, in her mid-to-late sixties. "I light this candle in memory of my son Mike, my entire life and my love. He was thirty-two when he died from cancer of his leg. He lost his leg when he was eighteen, and they thought the amputation would cure him, and he did well for years. Never missed the leg; he adjusted. We thought he was cured, because that's what they told us.

"But when he was in his mid-twenties he got pneumonia. Or, that's what they thought. And then they found out it was cancer from his bone tumor that got into his lungs. Then it was the chemo, worse than losing the leg. He had more complications, and couldn't take care of himself, so I moved into his apartment to help take care of him..."

"Denise?" The facilitator raised her finger and her eyebrows. "Can we continue your story in a little bit, so the others can introduce themselves and their children?"

"Oh, yes, of course." She looked at her shoes, contrite. "Sorry."

Next to Denise was a young man in his early thirties. All eyes turned to him, while he sat forward, elbows on knees, staring at the floor. He looked up and then looked at his wife next to him, handing her the candle.

"Hi. My name is Sandy. And this is Corey, my husband. Bethany was four months old. We thought she was in perfect health. So did her pediatrician. She was beautiful. Laughed all the time. She slept in our room. I breast fed her, because I knew it was healthier and better for her. She was a very regular eater, until... one night she didn't wake up at 4:00 a.m., like she always did. I woke up at 5:00, my breasts hurt so much, and I looked at the clock, and that is when I panicked. She was lying on her back. Her head was turned. Her lips were so blue. And her eyelids." The woman began sobbing, put her face in her hands. Corey looked at the floor. The woman on the side opposite her husband reached out and patted her shoulder.

"That was three months ago, and I still think I will wake up, and it will all be a nightmare. But it keeps going on. Every day. It seems like it's been all my life. We're still waiting to hear from the medical examiner. We still don't know why she died."

"All of us can see your pain tonight, Sandy. We are here for you." The facilitator's voice was even and calm. "Would you like to light a candle in memory of Bethany?"

"Yes," she sniffled, and she put her candle on the table with the other two. Corey continued to stare at his feet, leaning forward. But Erica could see him crying. The next two women told the stories of their children and lit their candles. They both seemed like they were regular attendees of the group.

A man with curly, black hair below his ears sat next to Erica.

"My name is Henry Schneider. I lost my son, Gerald, almost a year ago. He was seven years old, and he had an infection throughout his body, including his spinal cord. Meningitis. I light this candle in memory of Gerald."

Erica felt the group's eyes turn toward her, and her face warmed. She felt words choking her throat, and she could not speak. She gasped and shook her head, lit her candle and placed it on the table.

"It's okay, Erica." The facilitator filled the silence. "We all understand. You can talk when you feel like talking."

Erica was in a fog the rest of the evening. She heard people talking — about their children, their sadness and anger, their feelings about friends and family saying stupid things. The evening was mostly a blur, but the hour and a half passed more quickly than she'd have guessed.

The group stood as one and began to retrieve their coats from hangers in the entrance way. Several paused in small groups and continued talking in hushed voices, while others moved to the door. Erica looked out the window for her father's car when she felt a touch on her arm.

"I'm sorry for your loss." It was Henry, who'd been sitting next to her during the meeting.

"I am for yours, too."

After an awkward silence, the young man said, "If you'd like to meet for coffee sometime, I think we have a lot in common."

Erica stepped back in surprise. "Why... yes... of course. Sometime. That would be nice." And then, "My ride is here. I'll see you next month." She hurried out the door, where her father was just pulling into the parking lot. She climbed into the car and buckled her seatbelt.

"How was it?" He looked at her from his driver's seat.

"It was okay." He looked at her a few seconds more, then put the car in gear and drove back to the road, and they drove the fifteen minutes home in silence.

***

The support group met monthly. In addition, Erica was to meet with a "peer counselor" — another parent who'd lost a child, who would understand what she was going through. A woman named Valerie had been "assigned" to her. Erica was to meet with her later that first week. It was part of the agreement with her doctor when she was released from the hospital, just like the support group. She wasn't thrilled, but what choice did she have?

Her first meeting with Valerie was Thursday after the parent group meeting. And every Thursday afternoon after that for... she didn't know how long. But this was the first time, and she knocked on the office door.

"Come on in." Her voice was happy, upbeat. Sugary?

Erica opened the door. The office was lit with indirect and pleasant ambient lighting, and a floral scent from an air freshener floated lightly in the air. The woman sat behind a desk, but in front of the desk were two comfortable looking easy chairs, facing each other at a slight angle.

"Come in," the woman said, pointing at one of the two chairs. She rose from behind the desk and moved to the second of the chairs, stopping first to hold out her hand.

"I am Valerie. And you are Erica?" Erica nodded.

"Well, I am glad you've come, Erica. Please have a seat." Erica moved to the chair opposite the woman.

"Erica, first I want to tell you that anything said in this room is completely confidential, just between you and me. The only exception to that rule is this: if I become concerned that you might be thinking of hurting yourself or someone else.

"Second, I am here to listen to you, to let you express yourself and whatever feelings you might have. Crying is okay. So is anger. I will do my best to be non-judgmental. I am not a professional counselor, and I don't really give advice, though I may have suggestions based on my own personal experience and those of others I have known through the years.

Are you okay with all of that? Do you have any questions?"

Erica nodded her head yes, then shook it no, to each of the two questions.

"First, let me tell you about myself," the older woman continued. "I lost my baby when I was in my twenties. It was a girl. I was about 7 months along. The doctors couldn't explain why I miscarried. They said, 'this just happens sometimes.'

"That was fourteen years ago. July 17. I still feel like part of me is missing. My husband and I celebrate her birthday every year. Abigail. We call her Abby."

Erica listened without saying anything, without even nodding.

"We tried for a couple of years to get pregnant again, but it just wasn't meant to be." Valerie dabbed her eye with a tissue.

The two women sat facing each other at a slight angle. Erica's legs were crossed, and her foot bobbed slightly in the silence.

Valerie's sigh was barely audible. "How long has it been for you?"

Erica looked up. "Eight months and eleven days."

"What was your child's name?"

"Robbie."

"Do you feel like talking about it?"

Erica swallowed hard against the lump in her throat. "I don't really think so."

"You know, Erica, it is never easy to talk about your loss and the pain. It can be upsetting, but often you'll feel better afterward, just from getting it all out. And it helps to talk to someone else who's been through it. No one else can really understand what it feels like."

Erica's cheeks warmed. How can this woman understand? She had a miscarriage. *My 3-year-old drowned,* she thought. *He laughed, played, hugged, loved. He had his whole life ahead — starting school, playing soccer, his first girlfriend...* Then, guilt rose up from her belly, and she was ashamed of being mean-spirited, even in thought.

"I don't think I can talk about Robbie right now. Maybe some time."

The other woman frowned a bit, then recovered. "What about your family, your husband? Are they supportive?"

"My husband and I are separated. My parents don't want to talk about it. I think they are afraid of upsetting me, so they pretty much avoid it."

"Hmmm." Valerie nodded. "That is very common. Friends and family mean well, but they just don't know how to act. Or what to say. Is that like what you are saying?"

Erica looked at her palms, open in her lap.

"Yes." She looked up. "I guess."

"Do you get angry at your parents because they don't know how to act?"

"Not really."

"Why not?" the woman pressed.

"Why should I be angry at them? We are all just trying to survive, and none of us knows how to do that."

They talked a bit more, perhaps a half-hour. But Erica was in a fog again, and later could not remember much of what they'd talked about. But she was glad when the hour was over, and unsure what to say when Valerie said she looked forward to meeting again in a week.

She walked to the parking lot, and to her parents' car. They had been reluctant, but agreed to her driving alone for the first time. Though drained after her session, she felt fine, and she headed back to her parents' house. She had no time to waste. Story Hour began at 3:00.

***

"Hi, Mom."

"Hi, honey." She gave her daughter a peck on the cheek while toweling dry a glass from the sink. "How did it go?"

"I don't know. It was kind of weird. I'm not sure I liked it much."

Erica's mother put the glass up on a shelf in the cabinet and looked back. "What do you mean, 'weird'?"

"Can I tell you about it later? I have to get some things at the store before Story Hour at the library."

"Sure, honey. See you before supper."

Erica had volunteered for Story Hour at the branch library near their house. The program was designed to supplement kindergarten and pre-kindergarten activities in the area, and met three times a week. Erica had been volunteering for three weeks, along with two other volunteers. The three of them met with a dozen or so children ranging in age from 4 to 5, using a separate room inside the library.

They read pre-school level books, and Erica discovered her inner voice as an actor. She threw herself totally into the characters as she read. And she was surprised that the children were so attentive.

There were some other activities, as well. Coloring. Sometimes "sculpting" with Play-Doh. Erica was surprised that the children never seemed bored. They always seemed engaged, and that made her feel good.

When she started, she was very nervous. She worried that seeing children the age her own son would have been would prove too painful. And she was surprised that it was not. Though, sometimes, without warning, a child would run up to an arriving parent, and her throat would tighten, her eyes burn. But the Story Hour was good, and she looked forward to it.

During the days she wasn't preparing herself for meeting Valerie, or now thinking about the parent group, she was preparing for Story Hour. But there were other hours — many. And Erica read books, and she wrote. She began keeping a journal, and she wrote there every day, sometimes more than once.

Only one time did she go back and read what she'd written, three weeks' worth. She was surprised at the highs and the lows, and how closely they came together. She didn't quite remember them that way, but there they were, in her own words.

***

Two days after her meeting with Valerie, Erica was reading in her room upstairs when the phone rang. After a minute, her mother's voice echoed up the stairs. "Erica, it's for you," she called from the bottom step.

Erica went to the top of the stairs and asked silently, "Who is it?" Her mother shrugged, and Erica sauntered slowly down the stairs to retrieve the phone.

"Hello?"

"Erica? Hi. This is Henry." An awkward silent pause. "From the parent group?"

"Oh, yes. Hello, Henry. How are you?" And without waiting, "How did you get my number?"

He chuckled. "Well, I know your name. And I can be resourceful when I want something."

The hairs on her arm bristled. "And what is it you want?"

"Well... Like I said last week, I'd love to meet for coffee, or if you want, perhaps a glass of wine some evening. I'd just like to get to know you."

Erica dropped the phone to her chest, speechless. Not wanting to be rude, but bristling, on guard, she brought the phone back to her ear.

"I am flattered," she said in a slightly trembling voice. "But I don't know you."

"Precisely! That's why I was hoping you'd meet. So we could get to know each other."

Another short pause before she replied. "I don't know, Henry. I'm not sure I'm ready. I have a lot of things on my plate right now, and I'm still just trying to get by. Perhaps you could call again? In another week or so?"

She tried to strike a balance between indifference and polite, without deceiving.

"Sure. I'll call you next week... if that is okay?"

"Yes, perfect."

"Goodbye, then."

Erica hung up without saying more.

"Who was that?" she heard her mother bellow as she climbed back up the stairs.

"Nobody. Just a guy from the parent group."

***

Friday came and passed. Erica read books, her reborn passion. Her parents did... whatever it was they did. She knew her father liked to spend time in the garage, tinkering with his vintage TR-6. She wasn't really sure about her mother. The Story Hour was that afternoon, which passed quickly. Saturday was a barbecue with some neighbors, friends of her parents. And on Sunday, Erica's parents went to mass. Erica stayed home.

The weekend did have a few "trigger" moments. On Saturday morning, Erica was driving to the grocery store for her mother. As she turned the corner of her street, she saw on the sidewalk a red and yellow plastic "big wheel." Robbie had not even owned one yet, but seeing this one paralyzed Erica. She saw Robbie running in the front yard, his diapers drooping, nearly dragging.

She hit the brakes, and pulled to the side of the quiet neighborhood street, breathing fast and heavily. She could feel her heart in her throat. And in her head. And certainly in her chest. Might she die herself? She told herself to breathe, slowly... deeply... in, out. It was nearly ten minutes before some calmness returned; finally she was able to drive the few blocks to the store.

That night she slept like a she-bear in hibernation.

***

Monday morning arrived on quiet toes, and Erica woke up gracefully, fully appreciating the early, pre-morning sun that began to infiltrate her window through dainty curtains. She rose quickly, showered, and was downstairs before her parents were even awake. After ransacking the cabinets, she found a box of pancake mix, and she knew what she'd been looking for.

With no noise yet from upstairs, she began to prepare the pancake mix. She rescued some sausage patties, long forgotten in the back of the freezer, and she began to prepare breakfast. She poured measured coffee grounds into the coffeemaker, after filling it with water. And she flipped that on, just when she heard the sound of an upstairs flushing toilet. Her parents were awake.

Erica started the patties in an iron skillet on low, then began to search the fridge for syrup. She found a large squeeze bottle, and squirted a cupful into a small mixing bowl. It would have to be heated right before serving.

She heard a soft *pat ... pat ...* on the last steps from upstairs. She glanced aside, and her mother rounded the corner, in a long and fancy nightgown, or robe... Erica was not sure.

"Hi, Mom. I've started breakfast."

"It smells good already. Is that sausage? Where'd you find that?"

Erica shrugged.

"Is Dad gonna wake up?"

"Oh. He'll be right down. He's... in his 'library' reading educational materials." She grinned, and Erica returned the smile. "*New York Times*?"

Just then her father bellowed across the living area floor. "What are you saying about my reading habits? And what the hell is that sausage smell?"

"How 'bout a coffee, Dad? Straight up? Or blondish?"

"Straight up, girl. You know that."

She poured three black coffees, and put them before her parents and a third seat at the counter. Then she moved the sausages to the side of the skillet, and poured the batter in, making two perfect circles, not too large, not too small. When bubbles appeared on the top, she flipped them over gently to the other side.

"Mom? Would you microwave that cup of syrup for 45 seconds? Thanks."

Taking two of the plates, she placed one pancake on the first, and then the second on the other, and quickly arranged two sausage patties alongside on each plate. With perfect timing, Erica's mother returned the syrup at the same time Erica placed each platter in its place. "Here's the butter."

Erica returned to the stove, while her parents dove into their breakfast. More pancakes were passed around, and syrup. Erica skipped the sausage herself.

That was the beginning of a good day.

After she showered and dressed, Erica sat down at the small desk in her room and pulled out her notebook. She began writing about the weekend just passed. Only then did she appreciate how full it had been. She also began gathering materials for Story Hour that afternoon. Most of the books were at the library, but she'd brought a few home for preparation. She'd also bought a book about teaching children to work with their hands, using materials like clay, papier-mâché, and in their case, Play-Doh. She began studying, like a schoolgirl before an end-of-term test.

Erica lost track of time, suddenly realizing that she had to leave without eating lunch in order to get to the library by 2:00 p.m. She had to organize their room in the library, placing yoga mats on the floor for the children to sit on and putting the craft materials in order before the children began to arrive before 3:00. A few of the children arrived escorted by their hand-holding mothers. But most were attended by a nanny, recognizable usually by darker skin and a variety of accents.

Going into the fourth week of the Story Hour, Erica was starting to know the children individually. Mooshi was an outgoing and bubbly child; biracial, Erica guessed. She was precocious and "in your face." Olivia was the social butterfly, engaging each of the other children as often as possible. Ananya was quieter, a keen observer of everything happening. Her mother wore the traditional Sikh headdress, the *ghoonghat*.

Andrew was the quietest of the children. He was also the tallest, and Erica thought older than the others. He was brought by his Filipina nanny, who made up with her chattiness for Andrew's reticence.

The two hours, as always, passed quickly, the giggling of the children audible throughout, even through the closed door of their room. Parents and nannies began arriving around 5:00 to retrieve their children. By 5:10 the room was empty except for Erica, the other two volunteers, and Andrew, who sat distractedly playing with a golf ball-sized lump of Play-Doh.

Erica turned to the other two women.

"Why don't you guys go on? I'll stay here until somebody comes for Andrew." They thanked her, gathered their belongings and headed for the door.

Erica returned and sat on the mat next to Andrew.

"What are you doing there, bud?" she asked, pointing to the ball of Play-Doh. He continued to mash it with his fingers, not looking up.

"What are you making?" she asked again.

"A monster," came his delayed answer, still not looking up.

Erica persisted. "A monster? Is it a scary monster?"

The boy nodded.

"What does the monster look like?"

Surprisingly, the boy looked up. "A lump," he replied.

"A lump? I see... What are you doing to this monster?" She watched as he pressed his fingers into the lump of Play-Doh.

"I'm trying to kill it."

At that moment, the door to the room opened.

"I am so sorry I am late. I got tied up at work." A tall man with dark, thinning hair and the outline of a beard slightly more than a five o'clock shadow. "Am I interrupting something?"

"No." Erica stood up and held out her hand. "We were just killing monsters."

"Well, that's a good thing. I'm Jim, Andrew's dad." Andrew stood up and took his father's other hand while Jim shook hers.

"My name is Erica. I am one of the volunteers for the Story Hour."

"I had one of those 'really important' meetings at work. It lasted twice as long as it should have, and it wasn't really important at all."

Erica laughed. "Yeah. I know what you mean."

Jim stooped down to the mat and started picking up toys, cans of Play-Doh, crayons, and markers. "Here. Let me help you at least get cleaned up and get out of here."

Erica looked up curiously. He looked about forty, with slight graying around his temples. His jaw was well defined. His suit coat was opened casually, and his white shirt wide open at the collar. His eyes were kind as he attended to his clean-up. He tossed some Crayola's into the box, and looked up, and their eyes met.

Erica looked down. "I can finish up here, Jim. Thanks for your help."

"Oh, no. Thank you for being patient with my being late. I really appreciate it, and I promise it won't happen again." He stood up, and held out his hand.

"Erica, it's been a pleasure to meet you. And thank you again for watching Andrew a bit longer."

"Good night, Jim."

Erica watched as the father wrapped his son up in his jacket and, holding the boy's hand, walked out without looking back. Erica was still for a minute, looking blankly at the door, and then she felt tears well up in her eyes and begin to run silently, slowly down her cheeks.

***

Erica said hello to her parents, who sat watching the news on TV.

"There's some left-over pasta, salad, and garlic bread in the fridge. We weren't sure when you would be home, so we went ahead and ate."

"Thanks, mom. That's great." And Erica scuffed into the kitchen discovering that she was hungry, even if she had not felt it earlier. She found the pasta alfredo and scooped it into a bowl, then placed it into the microwave.

"How did it go today," her mother called from the living room.

"Oh, it was okay. The kids were good, and I think everyone had fun."

She paused, then added, "There is one boy who is different.

He is quiet. And his father comes to pick him up. Never his mother. Tonight, his father was tied up at work and was rather late, so I stayed to watch the boy."

"Oh, my. I wonder where the boy's mother is."

"I don't know. Maybe she works odd hours or something." *Or maybe something else*, she wondered.

***

Erica had few plans for the upcoming weekend. The only event was an all-girls night out on Saturday. A few of her friends from college days were getting together to celebrate one of their friends' birthday. Like Erica, the other girls all had married soon after graduation, and families began soon after. Most of her friends had at least one child. A part of Erica was looking forward to the evening, but another was filled with dread.

On Saturday evening, Erica donned a simple outfit of skirt, blouse and sweater, and added a light coat against the still chilly late-March evening temperatures in Baltimore.

"Bye, Mom. Bye, Dad. I won't be too late."

"Have fun, honey," came her mother's voice from the living room.

The gathering was at a Mexican restaurant about fifteen minutes from their house. Erica had no problems finding the restaurant and parked on the same block. Three of her friends were already seated and ordering drinks when she walked in. A basket of chips and bowls of salsa sat in front of them, and the girls talked excitedly. Erica walked up and, seeing her, two of her friends stood up to hug her. She sat down in one of the empty seats, draping her jacket over the back of her chair.

As one they were drawn back to the center of the table, and multiple conversations resumed simultaneously. Erica was not surprised that they were chatting excitedly about soccer games and babysitters. She ordered a margarita when the waiter returned with the other women's drinks. The others chatted excitedly about their lives, their memories of pranks and naughtiness during college years.

The waiter returned with Erica's drink and asked if he could take their dinner orders. They all ordered, and then it was Erica's turn. "I think I'll pass. Except for the chips." The others glanced at her, but no one spoke.

After the waiter left, the chatting resumed. Erica was quiet, vaguely listening.

"Erica, you're awfully quiet," one of her friends inquired.

"Yes. I suppose so."

And after a minute of silence, the others staring at her, she added, "I don't think I'm good company. I think I'll go on home." And she placed a ten-dollar bill from her purse on the table.

The next day was Sunday, and she again did not join her parents for church. Ever since Robbie's death, she had not been able to think about God without getting angry. She had no use for God anymore.

***

Tuesday was parent group again. Erica drove herself this time. She was a bit early. The blonde woman and her co-facilitator, Bob, were arranging the overstuffed chairs in a wide circle around the table in the middle. They both greeted her by name. She returned the greeting and took a seat. Soon others straggled in. It was the same group as the first time. She tried to remember their names — Barbara, Denise, Sandy and Corey. Just then, Henry walked in and took the seat next to Erica, smiling at her as he sat.

The group started and proceeded much the same as the first one. This time, however, Erica told a bit of her story.

"I'm Erica, and I light this candle for my son, Robbie, who died not quite a year ago from a swimming accident. He was four years old. I think of him every minute, and I don't know how I will last."

Henry reached over and patted her forearm. Erica drew her arm away.

The rest of the meeting was much the same as it had started. People talked about their month, the high points and low points. Once again, Corey said very little. Erica also said little more after her introduction. The others were mostly talkative, including Henry, whose voice sounded to Erica a bit whiny.

When the meeting concluded, they all began to leave for home. As Erica moved through the door, she felt a hand from behind on her arm. She turned, and she was not surprised to see Henry. He smiled.

"How 'bout that glass of wine. You got an hour or so?"

She felt less obliged to be polite this time.

"No, Henry. I am not interested."

"Oh. OK. Well, how 'bout I call you again this week?"

"No, Henry. I won't be interested then either." She turned and walked briskly to her car without looking back.

***

Erica decided to devote most of Monday's Story Hour to working with Play-Doh and Legos. She had thought about preparing a batch of papier-mâché paste, but it seemed too complicated for a short session. She was curious about using arts and crafts toward helping young children express themselves.

When all the children were sitting, Erica and her co-workers began explaining.

"Today we are going to make things that are our feelings, okay?

You can use Play-Doh, or if you want, Legos. How many want Play-Doh?"

A third of the hands went up.

"And so the rest of you would like Legos?"

Heads nodded.

"Are you ready to get started?"

And the three volunteers started distributing the materials, the Play-Doh and the Legos. When the children were settled, Erica said, "Let's all close our eyes, and think of what we feel, right now, at this moment. Are you happy? Are you sad? Are you afraid? Are you mad? Whatever you are feeling, it is okay. Feelings are good. And sharing feelings is a really good thing. So... What I want you to do is use your Legos or your Play-Doh, and make something that shows the rest of us what you are feeling.

"If you want help, just ask any of us."

The kids looked puzzled. Erica picked up some Play-Doh. She made three balls stacked on each other.

"What is this?" she asked the children.

"A totem pole?" one child asked?

"Bowling balls?" offered another.

Erica smiled, "Good ideas. But I was thinking that I am happy right now, and it made me think of making snowmen with my dad when I was your age. It made me happy. Just like now. With you guys.

"Who wants to try to make something with your feelings?"

They chorused, "Yay!" Then they began their individual work.

The three volunteers circled the children while they worked, offering advice and help. The kids seemed excited. Andrew? Not so much so. He rolled a ball of Play-Doh the size of a clementine, rolling it around and around in his hands, but not trying to shape it.

Erica saw him, sat down beside him on a mat.

"Andrew? Is that a monster?"

He nodded.

"Is it The Lump?"

He nodded again.

"Are you still trying to kill it?"

"Yes!"

"Why are you trying to kill the lump?"

"So it won't kill my mother."

Erica gasped. She understood. It was like being surprised by a violent thunderstorm.

"Andrew? Did your mother die because of The Lump?"

He nodded, starting to sniffle.

"Is you mother gone?"

"Yes, ma'am."

"I bet you miss her very much." He started to cry quietly. Erica put her arm around his small shoulders. "She knows you miss her. And she loves you very much."

Andrew stopped kneading the Play-Doh, and sat quietly. Erica stayed by his side, silent. She stayed there while the other children chattered about their creations with the other volunteers.

Finally, Andrew took the Play-Doh in his hands and started

breaking it down from a single ball. Soon he had three smaller balls, and he stacked them atop each other. When he was finished, he showed it to Erica, and looked at her.

"It's a snowman."

Erica's throat swelled.

"It's beautiful, Andrew."

The time had passed quickly and soon the parents and nannies were arriving to retrieve the children. Once again, Andrew was last. And, once again, Erica dismissed the other volunteers. When they'd left, she sat at the two-foot table with Andrew

"Andrew, I thought what you did today was fantastic. Did you kill the monster?"

He looked at the floor, silent.

"Did you feel good that the monster might be gone?"

Still, nothing.

"Andrew…Why did you make a snowman?"

"I felt happy."

"Did that feel good?"

"Yes, ma'am."

"I am so glad."

She wanted to hug him, but she knew that would not be appropriate. And at just that moment the sound of the door opening. It was Andrew's father, Jim. She was glad he was late and that she'd once again stayed late with Andrew.

"I am so sorry. I did it again. I am late. Again. I won't explain. It was a personnel problem I had to handle."

"It's no problem, Jim." She paused. "May I speak with you a moment?"

"Sure."

"Andrew was playing with Play-Doh again, the 'Monster,' the lump. We talked a bit. The first time he opened up at all. He told me that the monster, the lump, had killed his mother. That's why he wanted to kill the lump."

"Oh my God! He hasn't talked about his mother since she died! I knew he was upset, inside. But he didn't talk about it at all."

"May I ask what happened?"

"Of course. Claire was diagnosed with breast cancer... that's the lump, I guess... about two years ago. It was already Stage 4. She went through horrible chemo, and radiation. It was terrible. For me, for sure. But Andrew was there through it all, too. And he could not understand what was happening. I tried... but...."

"I understand," she offered. "I think he may be ready to talk more now." And, as an afterthought, "Do you think you are?"

He looked down at the floor, silent, for a full minute.

"No."

"I am so sorry."

He shifted feet nervously. "Thank you for your interest, and for taking care of Andrew as you have. I can't tell you how much it means."

"Jim. It has been a privilege to be helpful, in some small way."

He moved toward Andrew, who was still on the mat, molding his Play-Doh. "Andrew? Wanna go home?" Andrew looked up at his father, smiled. He stood and move closer to his father.

"Thanks again, Erica. You are a special person."

Erica wanted to say, "So are you." Instead, she said, "Have a good night." She smiled so no one saw.

FAIRBANKS

The airplane descended on Anchorage in mid-afternoon. The flight from Baltimore had been over ten hours, including a stopover in Minneapolis. She'd left at 11:30 a.m., and it was now nearly 6:00 Alaska time. That was nearly 10 p.m. by Erica's biological clock. She was glad to be soon on the ground again.

Erica gathered her luggage and walked to the shuttle bus area, glancing at a clock. It was nearly 7 p.m. She easily found the shuttle to the Comfort Suites motel on the airport grounds. After registering, she planned to eat dinner and go to bed. In the morning, her journey to Fairbanks would begin.

Awakened at 6 a.m. with the first light of day peeking through the drawn curtains of her room, Erica pulled back the covers. It was already ten her time. She went into the bathroom and prepared to shower. There was still time to catch the end of the complimentary continental breakfast. She needed coffee badly. After repacking her oversized backpack and her carry-on suitcase, she headed to the lobby for some yogurt and fruit before checking out.

The RV rental lot was about six miles away, and Erica waved down a taxi. When she arrived, she approached the young man at the counter.

"Hello. I have a camper van reserved."

"Good morning. What is the name?"

"Erica. Erica Stoltz."

"Yes. I see it right here. You've paid for a week in advance, so you're all set. I'll have one of my associates take you to your Roadtrek. He will go over everything about the vehicle with you. Then you'll inspect it together for any existing scratches, and you'll have to sign some papers. Then you're on your way."

"If I need to extend for more than a week, can I do that over the phone?"

"Yes. We've got your credit card on file, so just give us a call."

"Thank you," and Erica turned as another young man approached her.

"Miss Stoltz? My name is Ben and I'll show you your coach. Right this way. Let me help you with your bags. Have you ever traveled in a camper before?"

"Yes. My husband and I went on a three-week trip with my parents a few years ago. I learned all about the black and gray-water tanks, how to empty them, and all that."

"Good. This should be quick then." The young man smiled at her. He looked to be in his early twenties. He was cute.

The orientation to the van was over in less than fifteen minutes. It was equipped with a built-in GPS, and before leaving, Erica entered the destination, Fairbanks. Like magic, a map appeared on the screen. Hwy 1 to Hwy 3, then straight northeast all the way to Fairbanks. An easy six hours.

The Roadtrek was perfect. Barely longer than a regular van, it was easy to drive and park. Yet, it had a full bed, a small kitchen galley, and a wet bath — shower and toilet in the same space. It would give Erica the autonomy to go wherever she needed to go to try to find Robert, but she would be safe and comfortable.

Erica spotted a Safeway just before reaching Highway 1 and thought she should stop and stock the small refrigerator. Milk, fruit, cereal, hamburger, a loaf of bread …. and a six-pack of IPA. Then she headed back, and merged onto the highway. In two miles the van exited onto Highway 3, which would take her the six hours to Fairbanks.

The road was four-lane until about forty miles up Highway 3, where it became a well-paved two-lane highway, with strategically placed passing lanes. The scenery was not yet as beautiful as Erica had learned it would soon become, and she began driving routinely, lost in thought.

A month earlier, she had managed to call Robert's brother, James. Robert, after he and Erica had experienced problems in their marriage, had left abruptly to stay with his brother in Fairbanks. When they talked by phone, James told her that Robert had moved after two or three months and was living in a remote cabin north of Fairbanks.

They talked again a few weeks later, and Erica told James she was planning to come to Alaska and try to find Robert. He seemed okay with the idea. She began to make her plans, and here she was.

What will I say to him? she wondered. *What if I can't even find him?*

What if he is angry, and hateful? What if he blames me for everything?

She could feel her pulse rate speed up. Or so she thought. She had had dreams about this reconnection, and they were not pleasant. She was determined to make this happen, but also anxious.

An hour later she passed the turnoff to Takeetna, a small village that she had read about. The town was born around 1900 with the development of the Alaska Railroad. It started as a sawmill, trading post, and a cigar and donkey store. There was a saloon as well, so that miners could be as well-provisioned as their donkeys. Erica had done her homework.

The village was now home to nearly 900 people; it was on the National Historic Register, but was mostly a hub for adventurous tourists — hunters, fishermen, kayakers, and vagabonds. As she passed the turnoff, Erica thought whimsically of how she'd like to visit, but her mission was pressing.

The next landmark was another two hours' drive. She would pass the Denali National Park, where she would also not be able to stop. But if she were lucky, and the clouds were sparse, she might be able to get a good view of Mt. McKinley, now known simply as Denali, after the indigenous people's word meaning "the high one."

When the highway began its passage past the park, she could see the mountains to the west, and they were striking — which only made her again sorry that she could not stop. Instead, she passed through the village of McKinley Park, with a population of about 200 year-round inhabitants, most of whom depended on summer tourists for their livelihood.

During the long days of summer, Erica had read, McKinley Park burgeoned to a thousand or more with the influx of tourists. As she passed through, the importance of tourism was obvious. Cafés, restaurants, lodges, and campgrounds lined both sides of the highway. Most would be vacant by the time the temperatures dropped, and the three-quarter day-long hours of sunlight were replaced by equally long nights.

Erica's attention to driving was distracted by Denali, to the immediate west. The imposing beauty of this mountain, which lorded over the entire land, was impossible to ignore. But Erica's determination prevailed, and she drove through. Fairbanks was but two hours further.

As she began to approach, Erica turned off the highway toward the campground where she'd made a reservation. It was about an hour southwest of the city, in a wooded and remote area. When she arrived, she was surprised. The sites were private and nestled among tall pines. Each had a fire ring and a picnic table, as she'd expected, but it was nothing like the crowded and open KOA campgrounds she'd known from family vacations as a child and later, young adult.

Erica pulled up in front of the office, registered and got some helpful information about the grounds and the surrounding area, including about Fairbanks. It was nearly 5:00 p.m. local time, not even considering her four-hour jet lag. She was ready to get settled, eat dinner, and relax. She'd already decided not to call James until the next day.

When she got to her campsite, Erica began to set up. First, the electrical hookup to the 30-amp box, then the fresh water. She would wait to connect the sewer hose and use the holding tanks at first. Ten minutes seemed not too bad for a relative novice. She could not believe the beauty of her site. No other campers were easily visible. The pines reached skyward toward the stars, which would not appear until so late she would surely be asleep already.

The kitchen galley was small, but well equipped — a two-burner propane stove, microwave oven, small refrigerator. A small dinette was situated immediately behind the driver and passenger seats. The campground even provided internet and cable TV. She was certain she would not use the latter. But the internet would be useful for updating her parents on her progress, as well as accessing any other information sources she might need.

Supper would be simple. Rice, with ground beef crumbles and frozen green peas enfolded. She began cooking after connecting her iPhone to the Bluetooth-equipped sound system. And she cooked to the enchanting voice of Sarah McLachlan. Strangely, she felt more at peace than she'd felt in months, momentarily forgetting her impending plunge into the unknown.

Dinner was outdoors at the picnic table, despite the attacks of intrepid mosquitoes. Though it was more than an hour till sunset, the pines and the mountains' shadows hastened the dusk at the campsite, and also brought an early chill. Erica cut the binding on the complimentary bundle of firewood and arranged it in the firepit next to the table. The wood was dry, and easy to light. Soon the campfire smoke smell she remembered from childhood and the warmth of the blazing fire calmed her even more.

Erica sat at the table, staring into the flames, and her mind began to wander — thoughts of her husband who'd become a stranger even before he left for Alaska; her parents, and the vague distance she felt; the confused feelings she'd had for Jim, Andrew's single father. And then, unexpectedly, she flashed back to that Sunday afternoon, the barbecue at her parents, the panic when they lost Robbie and then found him at the bottom of the pool.

Erica shut the thoughts out, staring at the fire. Her hands were trembling, though she hardly noticed. She had managed to move on, but nothing was changed. Robbie was gone. He was dead. He was gone forever. She put her forehead into her hands and began to weep.

By the time Erica returned to the present, the Arctic dusk had arrived, the fire was mere embers. She was cold and tired. She gathered herself up, carried the dishes and herself back into the van, illuminated brightly by the efficient LED lights. She'd clean the dishes in the morning. She put the sheets and blanket on the bed in the back of the van, and moved to the tiny bathroom, where she peed and brushed her teeth. Finally, she stripped her clothes off down to her underwear, locked the door, turned off the lights and crawled under the covers. She had not opened even one beer.

***

Erica woke with daylight seeping through the curtains of the van. It was 5:30. She had slept well, but still felt spent. Pulling on a t-shirt, she climbed out of the bed and went to the bathroom, splashed her face and brushed her teeth. The next priority was coffee, and she set a pan of water on the burner and brought it to a boil.

It seemed still early, though early and not-early no longer seemed clear. She was still under the influence of jet-lag. A package of instant oatmeal seemed perfect. And, the coffee. And while she savored the cereal and the rich coffee, she began to think about the day.

She would call James. And hopefully arrange a meeting with him. Which might go well, or ...

She did not know James well. He was the best man at her wedding, but he seemed aloof. And they never really talked, despite what she thought were efforts on her part to communicate. She was disappointed, even if she was never certain of how close the Robert and James really were.

She was nervous about calling him. But the cell phone beckoned — no, commanded — that she make the call.

"James? This is Erica. I am in Fairbanks."

"Really? ... Where?"

"At a campground about an hour or so south."

"Okay. What are you going to do?"

"I am going to try to find Robert, and I need your help. I need to talk with him."

There was a pause, and then James offered, "I don't know how much help I can offer, but tell me what you need."

"Can we meet for coffee someplace, and talk?"

"Sure. There's a great coffee shop, McCafferty's, on Cushman

Street downtown. I can be there in an hour." James was a software developer and worked from home.

"Sounds great. Make it an hour-and-a-half. I'll meet you there."

"See you then. Ciao."

Erica pulled a clean shirt and underwear from her suitcase before trying out the wet bath shower. She turned on the hot water heater and waited ten minutes before stepping into the closet-like bathroom. She quickly wet herself and turned the water off while she scrubbed her skin with a soapy washcloth, then turned the water back on to rinse.

When she was dressed, Erica moved outside and disconnected the electricity and the water, and climbed into the driver's seat. "Navigate to McCafferty's Coffee Shop in Fairbanks." And the magic map appeared on the screen. Her campsite was in Nanana, about sixty miles from Fairbanks according to the GPS. She left the campsite and headed north on Highway 3.

The terrain was familiar. Flat plains immediately beside the highway, but mountains instead of true horizon. Erica gazed aside at the mountains. She'd never seen such land, such scenery as this, and she sighed.

She drove on another hour and arrived in Fairbanks. The GPS was cocksure of the directions, and he (or it) brought her to the front of an older, square building nestled among other, similar establishments. Erica found a parking space just a few feet away, and she approached the door.

I'm not sure I will even recognize him ... I am not sure what to say ...

She opened the door, and several bells hung above the door welcomed her. She stepped in and began looking around. There weren't many tables, and a man started waving. His beard was full, long and speckled with silver. Erica hardly recognized her brother-in-law.

James rose from the table and opened his arms, embracing her distantly. She was taken aback, and she recalled how distant he'd always been.

"How are you? How are you doing?" he asked as they sat.

"Surviving. Getting better. And you?"

"Oh. My life is simple. I get up, I work, mostly at home. I cook some, and of course I eat. Life is simple. And I am happy."

"That's great, James. You truly sound happy."

The two were silent, neither sure what to say.

"You want a coffee?"

Erica brightened. "Yeah. That would be great."

The two rose and walked up to the coffee bar.

"You go first," James said to Erica.

"I'll have a medium mocha please."

James added, "A large black coffee for me." He pulled some bills from his jeans pocket and pushed them toward the barista.

"Keep the change."

The two returned to their table and sat back down. And the awkward silence returned with them.

"So, you say you want to find Robert ... "

"Ah, yes. I think we need to reconnect, at least to wrap up some details. You know?"

"No, Erica. I can't know. I never lost a child. But I can try to help you find Robert, though I ain't promising."

"Any way you can help me, James, would be great."

James' brow furrowed. "I haven't seen Robert in near a year. When he came here, he stayed with me a couple of months. He never said much. Seemed really gloomy. But then he headed up north. Found himself a little cabin on a couple of acres near Livengood."

"Livengood? I never heard of it."

He chuckled. "No doubt. It's not much of anything. Used to be a gold mine in the early years of the 20th century. Now it's little more than a dozen or two homesteads. But now International Mines have moved in, and they're developing a new project. They hope to be mining for gold again, just like the old days, only higher tech. I heard there may be some new job opportunities opening up. If you like hard work and adventure, that is."

"Where is it?" Erica raised her eyebrows.

"About two hours north of here. Off Highway 2."

"Any idea where Robert's cabin is?"

He shook his head.

"I've never been up there. But it shouldn't be hard to find him. Just look for somebody. When you find someone, just ask. There's not even fifty people there, and they all know everybody and their business."

Erica sipped her rich Mocha coffee.

"James, I can't thank you enough."

He frowned again.

"You going to try and go up there? What are you driving?"

"I've got a Roadtrek van I rented. I can live very comfortably in it for weeks."

"You got some spunk, girl. Just be careful up there. Be sure you have a full tank of gas, or you'll be heading back to Fairbanks."

Erica pushed back from the table, stood and held out her hand to James.

"Thanks again, James. I think I'll go back to my campground. I'll sign out there and head to Livengood in the morning. By the way, was the living there ever good?" She smiled.

"No, ma'am. I don't think it's ever been much more that bone-breaking work for little money, little provisions. The few folks there make a trip to Fairbanks ever couple weeks or so to stock up on food and supplies. A lot of folks hunt and fish for their suppers, too."

They walked together to the door. James turned left, Erica right.

"Bye, James." Erica waved as she turned.

***

It was nearly suppertime before Erica pulled into her campsite. She quickly reconnected the electricity and the fresh water hose, which she first used to fill the freshwater holding tank in the camper. She went back inside and took a hamburger patty out of the freezer, along with some frozen French fries. She put the burger and fries into an iron skillet and lit the stove. As her dinner began to cook, Erica took two slices of bread from the bag and got a slice of cheese, some ketchup and mustard, and a can of beer from the fridge. She again paired her iPhone with the stereo system and began to play some R.E.M., music which was timeless to her. "Losing My Religion."

Sitting down at the small dinette, she retrieved a road map of Alaska. With her forefinger she traced Highway 2 from Fairbanks north, until she found the nearly microscopic print — Livengood. It seemed a straightforward drive with no complicated turns. She thought, as she turned the burger, that she would leave early in the morning.

After eating, cleaning dishes, she was still not ready to sleep. And she retrieved from her backpack a novel she'd just started. It was the story of two unmarried, older brothers, who ran a ranch in northeastern Colorado. She was completely drawn into the narrative, and she was eager to resume her journey with the two brothers and their many acquaintances. Propping pillows and turning on the reading light, she stretched out and read. Something she had not done in earnest in some time.

Erica startled herself awake. The light was on. She was curled on the sofa and chilled. She clutched the book against her belly. She checked the clock, and was surprised that it was 3:00 a.m. Annoyed with herself, she arranged the blankets and pillows on the couch, soon-to-be bed. She stripped to her underwear and bra, and burrowed into the blankets.

Erica was startled from sleep a second time, when the annoying alarm on her iPhone sounded at 6:00 a.m. She reset the alarm for 7:00. When the alarm sounded the second time, she wiped her eyes, crawled out of bed and pulled on a sweatshirt. Then she searched again for the switch to turn on the hot water heater. She needed a shower, but she needed coffee more. And she put water into a pan and lit the burner. She was glad for her French coffee press.

A cup of coffee lasted until there was water hot enough for a shower, and Erica headed right in. It was a tiny closet, a "wet bath," in which toilet, shower and small sink all occupied one space. The shower is attached to the wall, but it is detachable to be used as a hand shower, which was the only practical way shower in a camper van.

When she'd dried and dressed, Erica poured a packet of instant oatmeal into a bowl, added water, and placed it in the microwave. She reheated the water for coffee and made a second cup. After breakfast, she cleaned up and began the chore of disconnecting the van from the tethers of the campsite — the water and electricity. It was already nine o'clock. In half an hour, she'd paid her bill, and headed out to Highway 3 toward Fairbanks.

She stared ahead. *I wish I had time to thank James.* And her thoughts returned to the road and the upcoming three-and-a-half hour drive. She did not want to think beyond that. This leg of the journey was still cloudy in her mind.

Lost in her thoughts, Erica was surprised when the GPS voice announced that she'd arrived at her destination. Surprised because she'd seen nothing but a few decrepit cabins. No one walked along the highway, no one to ask, and she drove on a mile or so. Then, as she rounded a turn, a larger log structure appeared — the Wildwood General Store. She pulled into the parking area, immediately charmed by the log structure with wide chinking.

An "Open" sign hung on the front door, and Erica walked in to discover a quaint souvenir shop. There was a refrigerator with soft drinks and beer, and food to prepare cold cut sandwiches. A white-haired woman in her late fifties looked up from a table where she sat with papers scattered in front of her.

"Welcome. Can I help you?"

"Yes, ma'am. I like your shop. But I came to get some information. I am looking for someone."

"Oh. Who might that be?"

"His name is Robert Stoltz. I think he's been living here for a year or so."

The woman's smile faded. "And who might you be?"

"My name is Erica Stoltz. I am his wife."

Now the smile became a frown. "And what do you want him for?"

"He left me soon after our son died. That was back in Baltimore. He came to stay with his brother in Fairbanks. We were both so torn up. I guess he just needed to get away.

"We haven't talked in all this time. I just wanted to see how he is. And see if there is any chance we might get back together. Try to work things out, you know?"

The woman's face softened. She invited Erica to sit down with her at the table, and held out her hand.

"My name is Deb. Deb Carlson. I know Robert, but not well. Nobody does. He is a loner up here. Keeps to himself. Does some fishing and trapping. I suppose hunting, too. But he doesn't socialize much.

He knows when we get supplies brought in for our little store here, and he usually has an order of his own. He comes in every few weeks to pick up his order."

Erica leaned back in her chair. "I see. Do you think you could help me track him down?"

"I can tell you how to get to his cabin. It's about a mile off the highway, up about three miles from here."

"Oh, Mrs. Carlson, I would be so grateful."

The woman seemed much more friendly. "Would you like some coffee?"

"Oh, yes. Thank you."

Mrs. Carlson stood up and walked to a back room. In a few minutes she brought back two steaming mugs.

"If you don't mind my asking, what happened to your son? How old was he?"

Erica felt her throat tighten. She could not speak for minutes, fighting tears at the back of her eyes.

"He was three."

She took a breath. "We were barbecuing at my parents' house, having fun. We didn't see him. Somehow, he fell into the pool, without a sound. When we realized he wasn't running around, we panicked. No, we felt panicked. And we quickly saw him at the bottom of the pool. We did everything we could think of, and the paramedics did, too. But he didn't make it.

"It's been so hard to go on living."

Mrs. Carlson's face was contorted, and her eyes glistened.

"Oh, my dear. I am so sorry. How terrible."

The two were silent for a minute or two. Then, Mrs. Carlson spoke.

"How can I help?"

"You already have. You've told me how I can find my husband. I haven't seen him or talked to him in over a year. I don't know what I want, but I know that I have to connect with him, at least once more."

"You are a brave woman. Drive on up north about three miles, almost exactly. You'll see an unpaved road, stone, off to the right. It's woods. Follow that road about a mile. His cabin is the only thing up there. I don't have any idea if you'll find him, but that's all I know to tell you."

"Thank you so much, Mrs. Carlson. I can't thank you enough."

"Good luck dear. And God bless you."

The two shook hands, and Erica turned and left.

The road was rougher. This was the portal to the Dalton Highway. The rough stretch of the road from Livengood to the highway's destination of Deadhorse, the Alaskan "seaport" on Prudhoe Bay, in the Arctic Sea, and the origin of the Alaskan Pipeline. It is best known as a main character in the television show, *Ice Road Truckers*. The highway was lined with fir trees that reached high into the sky. The road was like a tunnel.

There was only one road to the right, and it was almost exactly three miles from the General Store. She turned off onto the gravel road and proceeded slowly. It was dark as dusk, the trees so high only a narrow strip of sky visible above. Erica was careful. She was not certain that the van was equipped for this sort of road.

In fifteen minutes, she rounded a turn and saw a small cabin. It had to be where Robert lived. The cabin was surrounded by ground covered with a deep layer of brown pine needles. Nothing adorned the door or the outside of the cabin. At the side, a large wrought-iron rack held a stack of wood logs stood five feet high, six feet wide. A small porch with a nervous roof fronted the cabin. Erica could imagine sitting on that porch at night in summer, staring at stars.

There was no sound from the cabin, no sign of anyone inside. All the same, she walked up to the door and knocked. There was no answer. She knocked again, louder. Still no answer. She was not sure what to do next. She was not going to give up, but she did not want to invade Robert's privacy unannounced.

The answer came in an instant. She could camp right there. She had everything she needed in the camper — food, warmth, comfort ... even music. She could stay there all night, or until whenever Robert returned. It was 4:00, and though sunset was still hours away, the towering forest made the scene like dusk. She returned to the van, locked the door, and lay down on the bed after retrieving her novel. But she was too wound up to read, so she returned to Sarah McLachlan. Soon she drifted into uneasy dreams.

She dreamed of Andrew, the child in her library "class." Of his monster lump, which she came to understand. The lump in his mother's breast. She lost her breast, and he lost his mother. She dreamed of Andrew's father, until she was awakened by a firm knock on her door.

Erica's heart jumped. At first she was frightened until she remembered where she was, and she knew it must be Robert. He must be wondering who the hell was parked in front of his cabin in such a fancy van.

She wiped her eyes awake, went to the door and unlocked it. The man before her barely looked like her husband. He was thin, thirty or more pounds lighter. He sported an unruly beard that extended nearly to his chest. He held in his hand a large basket, with two salmon, scarcely moving, each about two feet long.

"Robert?"

"Erica? Oh, my God."

"Hello. I'm sorry to intrude ... to invade your life here ... "

He was surprisingly calm. "Would you like to come in?"

"Are you sure?"

"Yes. Come in. Nice ride, by the way."

"Yes. A rental."

Robert turned and carried his basket into his cabin, leading Erica in.

The cabin was small. A kitchen. A small living area. An enormous wood stove. A small futon couch. And to the side, a small bedroom, and something of a bathroom with a compost toilet. No shower, but a small wooden tub.

"Have a seat," he calmly said, pointing to one of two chairs at a small table.

"Thank you."

"Would you like something to drink? I can offer some water."

"That would be nice, thank you." And he pumped a handle next to his faucet, and water began to flow. He brought two glasses to the table, and sat down across from Erica.

He seemed surprisingly relaxed. "It is good to see you."

"Really?"

A pause. "Yes."

"Robert, I feel lost." She was afraid to have spilled so much, so quickly.

She continued. "Not a moment goes by when I don't think of Robbie. Sometimes ... I see something that means nothing to me, except that it makes me think of him, and I break down."

The two looked deep into their water glasses. Finally, Robert spoke. "Me, too."

"Robert, I can't help myself. I tried to move on, but it doesn't work."

"No. I know. Even here, in isolation, in the wilderness, with only bears and geese and salmon for friends, there are 'triggers,' things that bring back that day like a real-time rewind. And I can't handle it. So ... I go fish. Or I go check my traps, hoping for a catch for dinner. And at night, I cry."

Erica's eyes began silently to tear. This was not the Robert she last knew.

"I stopped drinking, right after I moved up here. Everybody here drinks. A lot. I guess it's the isolation and the loneliness. But I knew that my survival depended on not drinking. So, I came up here. I've lived alone, with animals for my friends. Nature for my partner. And it has been good."

Erica was silent, stunned. This was a person — her husband — and she did not know who this person was.

"Robert, I'm sorry this has been so hard for you."

They were silent a moment.

"It has been for me, too," she added.

"I am tired. I think I will go back to my camper and sleep. I am glad we talked. And I am glad you were not angry that I invaded your private life here."

"Okay, Erica. Have a good night. I hope we can talk more in the morning. Oh ... if you have no dinner plans, would you like some grilled salmon?"

"I don't think so, Robert, but thank you. I think I just need to go and think. By myself. May I take a rain check?"

"Sure."

Erica got up and moved toward the door.

"Good night, Robert. See you in the morning."

***

Erica could see the sky above the tall spruces starting to lighten when she opened her eyes. She also saw blue-gray smoke coming from the metal chimney of the cabin. She'd slept in her clothes, so she got out of bed, used the toilet and washed her face. She laced her running shoes, got out of the van and knocked on the door of the cabin.

"C'mon in," she heard. And she opened the door. Robert was stooped before the open door of the stove fire. He was holding a large salmon filet on a wooden skewer over the flames. He looked at her. "Care for some breakfast?"

"It smells great. I'm starving. I didn't eat last night."

Robert used a fork to remove the fish from the skewer and placed it on a plate. With a large kitchen knife, he quickly sliced the fillet into two pieces. Then he took two hefty mugs from a cabinet near the stove, and lifted a metal pot from the top of the stove. "Coffee?" he asked. Without waiting for a response, he began pouring into the mug he'd set before her, finally filling his own cup. He said nothing more, but placed one plate with broiled salmon before her, then took a seat across the table.

"It's not much, but it's healthy. No toast and eggs up here. I hardly ever get bread."

"It looks great. And the coffee is wonderful." She began to cut a bite of fish. "Delicious!"

Robert took a sip of coffee and began to eat as well.

"How did you find me?"

"Well, it wasn't easy. I called James about a month ago. He told me you'd moved up here. Said he hadn't seen you in a year."

"That's true. I feel kind of bad about that. He was good to help me out for a while when I was pretty messed up. But I still don't get how you found me."

"Well, I knew how to find Livengood, though there wasn't much to find. I did find the Wildwood General Store. There was a lady there. Pretty rough at first. Silent type. I told her I was looking for you. At first she wouldn't tell me anything, but wanted to know who I was. Even when I explained that I was your wife, she wanted to know what I wanted you for. Very protective of your privacy.

"Then I told her my story ... our story, and she got much friendlier. She told me how to find your cabin, and here I am."

Robert shook his head. "Wow, that's quite a tale. But why did you come all this way?"

"I felt like I had to see you. To connect somehow."

"Why? Why did you want to do that?"

Erica stopped chewing her fish and looked down into her coffee cup. "I just felt I had to. To tie up some things." She paused. "To say I'm sorry."

He raised his eyebrows, surprised. "Sorry for what?"

After another pause, she answered. "Sorry for not being better. I was not a good wife anymore after Robbie died. I probably made things even worse for you."

"As I did for you," he replied.

They finished their breakfast in silence. Robert pushed his chair back and took their dishes to the sink.

"Would you like to go for a walk later? I can show you around a little. This is pretty magnificent wilderness, and I think you'll like it."

"That sounds great."

"I'm going to go out and check my traps. I'll be back in an hour or two. You'll be okay?"

"Oh, yes. I'm fine." She got up and moved to the door. "I'll see you later."

Back in her van, Erica sat at her small table and took out her book and began to read where she'd left off. She turned on her iPhone and began playing a "cool jazz" playlist. She took a deep breath and felt her muscles relax, calm.

She was still reading when a light tapping on the camper's door interrupted her. She opened the door. Robert stood outside a few feet away with a large snowshoe hare in each hand.

"Will you stay for dinner?" he smiled.

"Is that dinner?" She pointed at the rabbits.

"Yep. I make a pretty good rabbit stew. Just let me take them out back and skin them. Then they have to soak a few hours in cold salt water."

Erica frowned. "Where'd you learn that?"

"Oh ... you learn a lot of stuff from folks around here." He turned, left the rabbits on the porch and went inside the cabin, returning with the kitchen knife. Picking the rabbits back up, he moved to the back of the cabin. Erica went back to her book.

About one o'clock there was a tap on the door. Erica opened the door and stepped out.

"The rabbits are all dressed and soaking in salt water. You feel like exploring the wilderness?"

"Sure. Let me get a jacket in case it gets chilly."

Together they set off on a path heading northeast from the cabin. Once they were in the woods, the day darkened in the shade of the towering spruce and lodgepole pine trees. The ground was soft and yielding beneath the browning carpet of pine needles. Directly above, the sky was a bright blue skylight.

The two hiked on, in tandem and in silence. A loud scurrying to the side of the trail startled Erica. By the time she looked over, whatever it was that caused the commotion had vanished.

"Did you hear that? Did you see what it was?"

"Don't worry. It wasn't a bear. Probably a fox, or possibly a lynx. They're plentiful out here, and very elusive. Now, it is possible we might run across a moose or caribou once we get out more in the open."

Erica's mouth dropped open. "Are you kidding me?"

"No, but the caribou here are a bit smaller than they are up more north. There is even a chance we'll see a bear."

"What the hell do we do if we see a bear?"

He looked back at her and grinned. "Nothing. They don't have much interest in people, and if we do see one, it will probably be the rear end as he runs away. Same for moose and caribou. They care way more about foraging for food than they do about humans."

"Thanks. I'm so reassured." And on they trekked.

The trail was a slight incline, enough to challenge Erica's breathing. She paused.

"Robert, wait up," as she caught her breath.

Robert turned. "You okay?"

"Yeah. I just need a minute."

Robert took off the backpack he'd been carrying and took out a water bottle, handing it to Erica. "You never go out anywhere in the woods out here without plenty of water." She took a drink and handed the bottle back to him, and they started back on the trail.

Fifteen minutes later, Erica could see more light filtering through the trees, and the trail had begun to descend. In another five minutes the trail again rose a bit, and they found themselves, side by side, gazing down into a rapid brook — not quite a river, but larger and faster than a creek.

Erica stood transfixed. "What is this?"

"A creek."

"Okay. Does it have a name?"

"I don't know. Maybe ... probably. But I don't know. It's one of a whole bunch of creeks and rivers that drain into the Tanana River to the southwest. The Tanana is loaded with trout, and it's part of the breeding ground for a couple of species of salmon. Sometimes they migrate this far upriver."

Erica was speechless. The water tumbled rapidly over rocks, small waterfalls, with more still pools just below. "It's beautiful. Do you fish here?"

"Hell, yes. All the time. This is about half my diet."

She shook her head. "Amazing ... "

They sat, silent, on the bank overlooking the swirling waters. They sat for some time, gazing at the tumbling waters beyond their feet. Erica realized for the first time that she did not feel uncomfortable.

Robert turned to her. "You wanna head back? Dinner is going to take a while. Not because it is gourmet, but because it is a stew, and it takes some time."

Erica nodded. "Sure. And thank you for taking me here."

They rose, and began the trek back to the cabin. The way back was easier, with mostly a slight decline in the path. No moose, bears, or even fox on the return trip to the cabin. And little conversation. They were both lost in thought.

When they arrived, they stood before the van for a moment. Neither spoke, neither knew quite what to say.

"I have a lot of preparation to do for dinner. It's nearly 4:00 now, and I need to get to work with the stew. Dinner at 6:00?"

Erica climbed into the van. She felt the need to shower, and she turned the propane-fueled water heater on, gathered soap and a towel, and waited another ten minutes to let the water warm. She placed clean clothes on the bed, undressed and wedged herself into the small wetbath, pulling the curtain around her. Taking the handheld showerhead, she rinsed herself with short bursts, then soaped up, and rinsed. *So, this is what they call a navy shower*, she thought. Next she wet and shampooed her hair before rinsing it as well.

After she was dressed, Erica started playing music from her iPhone and lay back on the bed with her book. She was so engrossed in the story of the two Colorado ranchers, who'd by that time in the book taken in a pregnant teen, that she was startled when Robert again knocked.

"Dinner's ready."

"I'll be right there." She put her shoes on and climbed outside.

When she walked through the cabin door, she was assaulted by a savory aroma.

"Wow. That's the rabbit stew? It smells wonderful!"

"I hope it tastes equally so."

She sat at one of the places at the small kitchen table. Robert brought two glasses of water and set them down. Then he returned with two steaming bowls of thick reddish liquid with swimming chunks of potatoes, carrots, onions and meat. She took a spoonful and blew gently on it to keep from burning her mouth.

Robert cleared his throat. "Watch out for the bay leaves. I didn't take them out."

"Robert, where did you learn to cook like this?"

"Well ... When you're pretty much alone in the woods of Alaska, you learn. I learned about trapping and fishing, and also about how to prepare what I can catch, from people around here. There are some people who have lived like this all their lives, and they know a lot. And they teach a lot. Some are indigenous Inuits who came south from the subarctic north. Work was easier to find down here, and some took advantage to help their families back home.

"They came south, but they didn't forget their hunting, fishing and survival skills. And some were willing to teach white boys like me."

"Robert, I am so impressed. This stew is amazing." She paused, looking down into her bowl. He looked at her eyes across the table.

"Robert, you have changed."

"Yes. Yes, I have."

"What changed? What caused the changes in you?"

He frowned. "The same thing that changed you."

She looked at him, questioning.

He understood her unasked question. "The same thing that changed you. Robbie."

Tears filled her eyes.

Robert seemed willing, eager even, to talk. "When Robbie died, I thought I'd died, too. I didn't know how I could go on. Every night I went to bed, I prayed that I would not wake up in the morning. Robbie consumed every minute of every hour, of every day.

"I would go to the bathroom in the morning to pee and brush my teeth, and I would see him standing there, in the doorway, watching me. No one understood. No one wanted to talk about it. I had nobody. Not even you.

"And then I started trying to numb the pain. The drinking ... "

The tears streaked her cheeks.

"I knew I had to make a huge change. Break away from everything I've known. Not that I would ever forget Robbie. Not that I would stop feeling the empty hole in my heart. But when I got here, the pain became less powerful. I didn't feel certain that it would overwhelm me, suffocate and kill me. Don't get me wrong. The pain still comes over me, out of nowhere. It still feels overwhelming, but I know I've been here before, and I survived. And eventually it recedes.

"And then I go fishing ... "

They were both quiet for a long while. Erica took a sip of her water.

"Robert?"

"Yes?"

"Do you think you will ever come back?"

"What do you mean?"

"I mean, do you think you will ever come back? To Baltimore? Do you think we could ever try to make it work again? Between us?"

"Oh, Erica. I don't know. I haven't even really thought about it. My mind is too full of other stuff to even think about that."

"I understand."

"Do you think you could consider a move here, to Alaska?"

She sat up in her chair.

"Well. I haven't thought of that at all. I haven't ... haven't ... I don't know."

They sat silently looking at each other. Outside, dusk was settling.

"Robert, I am exhausted. I think I am going to hit the sack early. The dinner was extraordinary. Thank you so much. You were a perfect host."

They both pushed their chairs back and stood up, Erica moving to the door, Robert following.

"Erica? Think about it." And he leaned forward, kissed her gently on the cheek.

"Good night, Robert."

"Good night, Erica."

She went back into the van and sat at the kitchenette table. Elbows on the table, forehead in her hands, she began to weep, silently.

She wasn't sure how much time passed, but outside was now completely dark. She brushed her teeth, peed, and crawled into her bed, falling almost immediately asleep.

When she awoke, after a dreamless sleep, it was already light outside. She was hungry again. She didn't hear any movement outside and wondered if Robert were awake yet. *Of course,* she thought. *He gets up before the sun, I'm sure.* She dressed and went to the cabin door, knocked.

"Come in."

She pushed the door open.

"Hi. I just woke up. I was going to make some oatmeal. Would you like to join me?"

"Oatmeal? Hell yes!"

"No bacon. No eggs. Just oatmeal... And coffee."

"Sounds great. Give me five minutes and I will join you in your ... uh ... cabin. Okay?"

"Sure. I'll get the coffee going."

Erica went back to the camper and started boiling the water for the coffee and the instant oatmeal. The tap on the door was not surprising.

"Come in," she called.

Robert opened the camper door and stepped in.

"Hey. Nice digs!"

"Have a seat," she pointed at the dinette. "It's just instant oatmeal. Quaker Oats. Maple/cinnamon."

"Sounds great."

"The coffee, though. That's the real thing. Kaladi Brothers out of Anchorage." She poured the hot water into the French Press with the coffee grounds, and after letting it steep for several minutes, pressed the grounds to the bottom. She poured Robert and herself a cup. Then she opened the two packets of instant oatmeal and poured them into bowls, followed by more hot water, stirring as she poured. She placed the two bowls on the table with spoons, and sat down opposite Robert.

"That was a really good dinner last night, Robert. Thank you."

"It was my pleasure."

"I think I need to head back home."

"So soon? No. I get it. This is a whole lot to process."

"Yes."

Erica took a deep breath. "Robert, I am glad that we reconnected. I feel more oriented than I did before coming out here. But I also feel confused. More confused."

"I know. I feel the same."

"You have salmon and snowshoe hare. I have new interests, jobs, as well. I need to rethink my life."

"I understand."

"I am going to leave soon. Get back to Anchorage and then on to Baltimore."

"I understand." A silent pause ... "I will miss you."

"Can we stay in touch? Do you even have a phone? E-mail and internet?"

"No. None of that."

"Why am I not surprised?" she asked, with a touch of irony in her voice. "So, how do we stay in touch?"

"I have a post office box in town. I can give you that."

"That would be great." She handed him a notepad and pen to write the address down.

"Robert, I think I need to go."

"I know."

***

Erica took her seat and fastened her seatbelt. In a few minutes, the attendants began their safety instructions in mime. Erica pulled the book from her backpack, and began to read again, even before the plane left the tarmac. She was soon immersed in the story of the two elderly brother ranchers, and their fumbling efforts to make this outcast, pregnant teenager feel comfortable in their home, her new home.

The flight was due to depart in ten minutes. It was just after 10:00 Alaska time. The flight was nearly eighteen hours, with two stops — Minneapolis and Atlanta. Erica would be doing a lot of reading and a lot of napping. And a lot of thinking *en route*.

ACKNOWLEDGMENTS

I would like to acknowledge the editors of the following publications for their support of the following stories:

"Trip to St. Vitus" (*Caravel Literary Journal*, Winter, 2016)

"Salvation Army" (*Down in the Dirt*, June, 2017; *Random Thoughts*: *Anthology*, August, 2017))

"Bus Ride to Minot" (*Scarlet Leaf Review*, October, 2017)

"Asystole" (*Fixional*, Autumn, 2017)

"The Kid and the Poet" (*Inwood Indiana*, Autumn, 2018)

ABOUT THE AUTHOR

Greg Stidham is a pediatric intensivist (intensive care unit physician) who retired in 2012 after a 32-year career in academic medicine. In retirement, he has resurrected his passion for literature and creative writing. He has published a memoir, numerous pieces of short fiction, and creative nonfiction. But his real passion has been and is poetry.

Dr. Stidham grew up in Cleveland, Ohio, and attended the University of Notre Dame in South Bend, Indiana. He graduated with a degree in English while completing prerequisite courses to attend medical school. He received his MD and pediatrics training at the University of Toledo College of Medicine in Toledo, Ohio, before continuing his training in pediatric critical care medicine at Johns Hopkins University in Baltimore, Maryland.

Following his training, Dr. Stidham joined the Department of Pediatrics at the University of Tennessee Health Sciences Center and LeBonheur Children's Medical Center in Memphis. He started the Critical Care Program at LeBonheur and was Chief of the Division of Critical Care. Later in his tenure in Memphis, he started the hospital's Pediatric Palliative Care Program and chaired the Biomedical Ethics Committee for more than a decade.

After twenty-eight years at the children's hospital in Memphis, Dr. Stidham moved to Kingston, Ontario, where he assumed the position of Professor of Pediatrics at Queen's University and Kingston Health Sciences Center. He currently serves as a volunteer grief counselor for bereaved parents through Bereaved Families of Ontario. He continues to live and write in Kingston with his wife, Pam, and Dexter, the last survivor of their ever-evolving pack of rescue dogs.

An accomplished writer, Dr. Stidham has published a memoir, numerous pieces of short fiction, and creative nonfiction. But his real passion is writing poetry.

His books include the memoir, *Blessings and Sudden Intimacies: Musings of a Pediatric Intensivist* (PathBinder Publishing 2021), and a poetry chapbook, *Doctoring in Nicaragua* (Finishing Line Press 2021).

www.ingramcontent.com/pod-product-compliance
Lightning Source LLC
LaVergne TN
LVHW011943070526
838202LV00054B/4770